"Miss Dane…is there a chance that you may be pregnant?"

Aria stared at the pretty blonde doctor who sat perched on the opposite end of the low coffee table in the suite's living area, where the dawn light had just begun to filter in through the windows. She blinked, half thinking she'd misheard the question. It was absurd. She was vaguely aware of Nysio's swift intake of breath nearby but couldn't muster the courage to look at him.

"No, *no*… Definitely not."

But as she sat in choked silence, her subconscious continued to analyze the past week and how *different* she'd been feeling. The food aversions, the vague nausea she'd thought was anxiety, the tender breasts, even feeling more exhausted than usual.

"It might be a possibility," she said hoarsely, the last word coming out as a whisper.

"Cosa?" Nysio frowned at her with confusion, then straightened abruptly. "You think…you might be…"

"No," she said quickly. "Well…I shouldn't be."

"But you might be." He stared at her, his gaze unflinching, the sharp tilt of his brows utterly unreadable.

The Greeks' Race to the Altar

Claiming their legacy...or their wives?

The Mytikas family has long been surrounded by secrets and legend. Even in death, patriarch Zeus has every intention of making sure it stays that way.

He leaves one final challenge to his three would-be heirs... The one who makes it down the aisle first will inherit *everything*!

The race is on for these Greek billionaires— but soon it's about so much more than fulfilling the terms of the will... It's about claiming their convenient brides!

Discover Eros's story in
Stolen in Her Wedding Gown

Read Xander's story in
The Billionaire's Last-Minute Marriage

Check out Nysio's story in
Pregnant in the Italian's Palazzo

All available now!

Amanda Cinelli

PREGNANT IN THE ITALIAN'S PALAZZO

HARLEQUIN®
PRESENTS™

Recycling programs for this product may not exist in your area.

ISBN-13: 978-1-335-58411-3

Pregnant in the Italian's Palazzo

Copyright © 2023 by Amanda Cinelli

For questions and comments about the quality of this book, please contact us at CustomerService@Harlequin.com.

Harlequin Enterprises ULC
22 Adelaide St. West, 41st Floor
Toronto, Ontario M5H 4E3, Canada
www.Harlequin.com

Printed in U.S.A.

Amanda Cinelli was born into a large Irish Italian family and raised in the leafy-green suburbs of County Dublin, Ireland. After dabbling in a few different career paths, she finally found her calling as an author upon winning an online writing competition with her first finished novel. With three small daughters at home, she usually spends her days doing school runs, changing diapers and writing romance. She still considers herself unbelievably lucky to be able to call this her day job.

Books by Amanda Cinelli

Harlequin Presents

Resisting the Sicilian Playboy

Monteverre Marriages

One Night with the Forbidden Princess
Claiming His Replacement Queen

Secret Heirs of Billionaires

The Secret to Marrying Marchesi

The Avelar Family Scandals

The Vows He Must Keep
Returning to Claim His Heir

The Greeks' Race to the Altar

Stolen in Her Wedding Gown
The Billionaire's Last-Minute Marriage

Visit the Author Profile page
at Harlequin.com for more titles.

This one is for the big girls

PROLOGUE

NYSIO BACCHETTI WAS rarely surprised.

He was the sole heir to an Italian dynasty that dated back to the Renaissance, and the majority of the milestones in his privileged life had been mapped out from the moment he was born. From his elite boarding-school tuition to the prestigious business degrees that hung upon the walls of his office where he ran their family's sizeable estate and holdings, his life always tended to follow a neatly predictable path.

Until today.

Nysio forced himself to breathe, his eyes blurring as he reread the first page of the last will and testament of a man he'd never met. A man who was apparently his biological father, according to accompanying DNA test results dating back twenty years. The neat black envelope had been hand-delivered at noon by a representative of Mytikas Holdings. The sensitive details within had been briefly explained, along with an invitation to come to New York to discuss matters further with Zeus Mytikas's oldest son, the new CEO.

His brother. He had a brother.

He had *two* brothers, he'd discovered upon voraciously reading through the remainder of the shocking documents and turning to the Internet for more information. There was the stern-faced business mogul Xander Mytikas, the oldest son, and the one whom Zeus had apparently chosen as his protégé. Then there was Eros Theodorou, a laid-back blond playboy with a scandalous reputation. Both of them had the same blue eyes and sharp cheekbones as his own. Features apparently given to them by the biological father they shared.

All three of their names had been listed in Zeus's last will and testament. Not an offering, but a competition. The first of them to marry and remain married for one year...would inherit the entirety of Zeus's estate. It appeared that iron-clad legal bindings had forbidden Zeus from revealing the Bacchetti secret—that Nysio was apparently not a Bacchetti by blood—or using it against them. Until now. It seemed the old tyrant had decided to throw up one last middle finger from beyond the grave.

He found himself pacing the length of his office, throwing open the nearest doors and stepping out onto the terrace like a drowning man. The lights of the city spread out below Palazzo Bacchetti like a glittering blanket, taunting him.

The people of Florence lauded the Bacchetti family as their own unofficial royalty, and Nysio had grown up as their raven-haired prince, trained to perform his part to perfection, no matter what was happening behind the closed doors of their mountaintop *palazzo*. They were more than just a wealthy family, his elderly father often reminded him whenever Nysio dared to complain. They were an institution. And institutions needed to maintain their image to project stability to the people who relied upon them.

But now he knew better than anyone that the people who seemed most perfect were simply the ones who possessed the most secrets.

He had no need of any paltry inheritance. He had amassed more wealth at his computer trading stocks than the Bacchetti name alone could have ever given him. It was public knowledge that he was a recluse who rarely left his palatial compound in the Florentine hills. But unlike some of his ancestors, he had never needed public adoration or intimidation to keep his business in perfect working order, not when his patience and instincts as a financial trader were world renowned. Even on the most tumultuous days in the global stock markets, he had remained calm and in control.

But as he stared down at the documents he still gripped in his hands, he felt the edges of his hard-won control begin to fray with every breath he forced into his lungs.

Arturo Bacchetti was a good man and the only father Nysio had ever known. He had been trained with the sole purpose of taking his father's place as a public figure, despite the social anxiety that made many of his duties almost unbearable. He had dropped all of his own plans and stepped into that duty much earlier than planned, when his father had become ill and his parents had retired to Sardinia.

He had given his whole life to this city, safe in the knowledge that it was his birthright. That it was his duty. But all along his parents had been hiding this from him. The temptation to lash out was strong, but he had never been one for outward displays of emotion. He preferred to wait, to analyse, to plan his actions. And that was exactly what he would do, he decided as he strode back into his office and grabbed the phone from his desk.

Gianluca, their family's most trusted employee answered promptly, used to playing the part of Nysio's assistant on occasion among countless other jobs he took charge of. The older man was stunned to hear him request a jet to be readied for immediate travel but he gave no details other than to say it was a business trip. There was no need to disclose any more than that. No need to alert his parents, or speak of any of this at all. Zeus Mytikas had broken a legal promise to keep this secret under wraps, dead or not, and Nysio intended to ensure that the current CEO of Mytikas Holdings knew exactly where the Bacchetti family stood on the matter. He would regain control of the situation, have his name struck from that damned will and walk away. One quick trip across the Atlantic and things would go back to the way they were.

He would make sure of it.

CHAPTER ONE

WHAT AN UTTERLY dismal location for a wedding. Nysio scowled as his car came to a stop amongst the growing crowd that had gathered outside the grey brick Manhattan courthouse. The groom stood in their midst, stony-faced and proud even as he watched his bride-to-be turn tail and run, disappearing into the busy city streets.

Cameras flashed immediately upon the scene, and Nysio felt his body tighten in sympathy at the familiar invasion of privacy, even though he was tucked safely behind tinted glass. He studied Xander Mytikas from afar, curiosity making him analyse the strong nose and harsh brow that were so eerily similar to his own. For much of his flight across the Atlantic he had wondered how it might feel to meet one of his two half-brothers in person.

Wondered if he might feel a sense of kinship or connection.

The fact that he felt nothing should be a small relief.

So far, his team of private investigators had already uncovered no effort on either of his brothers' parts to sabotage his privacy. In fact, they had both seemed far too involved in their own private dispute to even consider that their surprise Italian counterpart might make an appearance. They both knew of his existence, they had all received the exact same document...and yet, other than having that copy of the will sent, they had not tried to contact him or acknowledge his existence at all.

Before he could think of his next step, Nysio could do nothing but watch as his brother cut through the crowd and disappeared into a limo down the street. Clearly, Xander Mytikas was not planning to sit around waiting to see if his runaway bride returned. The acting CEO needed to marry fast in order to keep control of his shares in Mytikas Holdings and, according to Nysio's investigators, he had no plans to reveal the previous terms of the NDA that protected the secrecy of Nysio's birth.

A flash of pink caught his attention, jolting his attention back to the street. A woman emerged out onto the courthouse steps, a shaft of sunlight illuminating her red hair into an amber glow against the dull grey stone of the building behind her. The chilly autumnal breeze blew her pink gown tighter against her, seemingly outlining her shape for his further perusal. She had flowers in her hands and shock on her beautiful face and Nysio was stunned to silence for a moment, thankful for the privacy windows so that he could look his fill.

From a distance, she reminded him of one of the ancient goddesses in the paintings in the gallery of his Florentine *palazzo*, as if she should have been in repose with cherubs feeding her grapes. And her *breasts…* He bit his lower lip, forcing down the jolt of arousal that shot through his solar plexus.

Stunned at the reaction her presence had evoked in him, he tracked her progress as she moved down the street, calling out for the runaway bride. She turned back, the expression on her face one of absolute confusion as the rain poured down and splashed up against her bare legs and the pale pink material of her dress.

Most of the press in the street had dispersed now, but the woman in pink lingered. Such fierce emotion emanated from her, he found himself powerless to look away.

She approached the remaining security guards, her hands gesturing wildly as she spoke. The vague sound of a lyrical British accent reached his ears as he strained to make out the conversation. Her expression changed from pleading to furious as the men got into their car and drove away too, leaving her alone on the concrete steps in the rain.

Nysio watched as she dug around in a tiny purse hooked onto her wrist and heard the distinct sound of her guttural curse as she came up empty. Then, for the first time since she'd emerged onto the street, she went completely still. If he'd been struck speechless by the strength of emotion passing through her when she realised the bride was gone, this sudden deflation was even more provoking. She looked around the street for a moment, then ducked back under the portico for shelter from the rain.

Maybe it had been her clear distress moments before or maybe it was the delicate shiver that passed through her voluptuous frame as she tried to hug herself against the chill but, before he could rethink it, he stepped out from his car, opening his own umbrella against the downpour.

Aria Dane clutched the mud-covered skirt of her dusty pink bridesmaid gown and shivered, once again wishing that she'd had the foresight to design a matching coat to shield her from the October weather. The delicate satin and tulle gown had been a flamboyant last-minute choice, back when she'd assumed she would be standing and posing for pictures for the majority of the afternoon, not running through Manhattan in the pouring rain in pursuit of a runaway bride.

She checked her phone once again, waiting for a response from the recently departed billionaire groom's security team. They said that Priya had probably just got cold feet but she knew her friend. She knew that something was very, very wrong.

She looked up at the old stone courthouse with its windows glowing orange in the rapidly fading evening light. She had made a few calls to the places she thought Priya might have run to, only to come up empty. Now she was stuck at the scene of the crime, so to speak, with less than five dollars left in her tiny clutch bag and no way of getting home. The sense of abandonment was strong and deeply triggering, but she refused to let her mind wander back to the one other time she'd found herself discarded by someone she trusted in a strange place.

She banged on the tall oak door of the historic building, not surprised to find the venue had been closed up. It was Sunday evening and the space had only been booked exclusively for the wedding, after all. The rain still fell in a light shower, the streets glistening under the feet of pedestrians. She stood frozen in her spot under the portico, her mind whirring over her options. Her flight home to London was due to depart in a few hours and all of her possessions were locked inside Priya's apartment. Including her passport, her ticket and the tablet computer she used for work. She froze, feeling panic and worry break through the first rush of adrenaline.

She was stranded.

Aria had long ago accepted that she was a natural helper, the kind of person who saw a problem and jumped into action without a thought. And yet every time she was in trouble herself, she always found herself alone. Like right now.

She looked at her phone once again, feeling her stomach twirl. She was going to miss her flight and that meant missing her opportunity to give the presentation that she had been working on for the past month. The one constant in her life over the past ten years was her job as a fashion buyer in one of London's largest department stores. She'd walked through the doors as a college dropout and worked her way up to a place where she now actually had some creative input on what went out on the floor each season.

In fact, over the past few years they'd even supported her as she undertook an online textile degree at evenings and weekends and relentlessly pitched her ideas to expand their minuscule plus-size lingerie section. She swallowed past the knot that formed in her throat. With all of the downsizing that had swept through the departments lately, she *really* needed to get home.

She briefly considered calling her parents for help and fought the swift wave of discomfort that followed. Being an outspoken, spontaneous creative in a family full of very calm, very organised accountants was hard enough without the fact that, unlike her three older sisters, she didn't earn a six-figure income. She barely earned enough to pay the rent on her studio flat in Richmond as it was.

None of them would be surprised that she needed help, of course. It had been more than a decade since her own ill-fated elopement, but her parents still saw her as the foolish daughter who'd found herself abandoned on a Greek island by her spoilt, rich boyfriend.

She was the last person who could judge anyone for an impulsive jaunt into matrimony, but the moment Priya had asked her to travel to Manhattan to support her through a last-minute marriage of convenience with a stranger, her intuition had screamed at her. She'd felt a soul-deep sense of unsettlement about the arrangement, but put it down to knowing this marriage meant Priya had to leave London.

There were a great many things in life that she was not sure of, but the intention of never entering into matrimony with another person was one that she'd thought she and her best friend had shared.

A low tinny whistling noise made her jump and it took her a few moments to realise that the noise was coming from the phone she'd stuffed into the bodice of her dress.

She hissed a greeting, the past ninety minutes of adrenaline making her hands shake even as she fought to keep her voice civilised.

'Relax. I'm fine. I'm safe.' Priya's voice was strangely breathless, her words uncharacteristically quick and clipped. 'I… I found another way to solve my problem but I need to leave town for a few weeks.'

Aria pressed her lips together, silencing the instant exclamation of disbelief on the tip of her tongue. First her calm sensible friend had run away from a wedding that would have solved all of her problems, then she suddenly had to leave town for a few weeks...? Priya *never* made spontaneous plans, she hated breaking routine.

'Another way? Another groom, you mean?' Aria asked, her heartbeat pounding loudly in her ears as she tried to think of what she needed to ask Priya to ensure her safety. 'Where are you going? Where is he taking you?'

Priya's voice was hesitant as she explained, as if she couldn't speak freely, but she was adamant that she was safe. It was obvious that whomever she was accepting help from was with her, standing nearby. Definitely a man. Yet another out-of-character action for her best friend. They both had their own issues with trusting the opposite sex, it had been what drew them together in a college bar as they'd bonded over stories of their disastrous first attempts down the aisle. They trusted one another with the hard stuff, or at least they had.

Her fingers tightened on the phone's hard case. 'I don't like this. I don't like any of it.'

'I don't like it either, but it's what I need

to do.' Priya's voice cut off for a moment, a strange tapping sound coming from the background. When she spoke again her voice was calmer. 'Look, it will all be fine. I'll explain everything once I'm back.'

Suspicion clouding her senses, Aria whispered into the phone. 'If you can't talk, just say yes or no. I heard Xander sent guards in pursuit of his brother…there was this one really intense, dark-haired man. Are you with him?'

The line went dead.

Aria chewed on her nail, feeling a pinch as she bit her skin. She had begun to pace at some point, a habit of hers when she felt restless, but when a throat cleared nearby, she realised she was no longer alone.

She fought to hold in the strange reaction that caught in her chest as she took in the man standing a respectable distance away from her. The same man she'd seen earlier, watching from a car across the street as the scandalous wedding unfolded. Working in the fashion industry, she was no stranger to beautiful men, but this man wasn't just handsome…he had the kind of magnetic presence and other-worldly good looks that made him stand out. His swarthy tan and silk pocket square made him look like a movie star from another time.

Was this the brother that Priya's erstwhile groom had seemed so frantic to find? He would fit the bill for the wealthy Mytikas family—everything about him seemed to scream wealth and privilege. Passers-by gave him a wide berth, some even stared as though they knew they were observing someone important…someone of power. And yet, when she gave herself a moment to look at him in detail, she could practically feel his discomfort as he barely tolerated the attention. He reminded her of a lion in captivity, one who had been tethered and seemingly tamed but…still vibrated with a fierce primal energy obvious to anyone who looked beyond the polished surface of his designer suit.

He was looking directly at her, his eyes scanning along the mud splatters that now painted her sheer stockings, as though the sight irritated him. He had stopped at the end of the steps and she was intensely aware that she was a woman standing alone on a quiet street… yet she strangely didn't feel any fear. In fact, she seemed to be waiting for him to speak, her breath held and her body leaning ever so slightly forward.

His gaze met hers for a split second and for a moment she stood frozen, her body enthralled under the laser focus of stormy blue eyes and long lashes. It was an assessing glance, barely lasting more than five seconds or so before he looked away, but Aria instantly felt her heart thundering in her chest.

'Do you require assistance?' he asked in heavily accented English.

'What gave me away?'

'I saw what happened with the wedding. You are a friend of the bride and groom?'

Aria paused, noticing the way this man was very deliberately trying to seem nonchalant in his questioning. He could be a reporter, trying to get a scoop. She paused to set him straight, but they were both startled by the sudden blinding flash of a camera exploding against the dull grey concrete around them.

Aria inwardly groaned. She had spent so much time protecting her socialite best friend from the paparazzi and she had no wish to answer any invasive questions about the failed wedding. Especially since Priya was still missing.

But the photographer disregarded her completely, their focus solely upon the mysterious man at the end of the steps. 'Nysio Bacchetti, what are you doing in Manhattan?'

The man, clearly shocked at being addressed

by name, began to walk away towards the side of the building, but the reporter was relentless, caging him with questions and snapping photo after photo.

'Hey, leave him alone,' Aria shouted, only to be thoroughly ignored. The rain fell down upon her as she stepped out from the portico and ran down the steps. 'I said leave the man alone, for goodness' sake.'

The paparazzo scowled, stopping only to press a few buttons on his camera then turning back to continue his photographic assault. A single wheezing breath sounded out loud over the soft patter of rain around them. The gorgeous man in the fancy suit had stopped retreating and was now frozen in place, half leaning against the thick branch of a tree as his breaths came hard and fast.

'What did you do to him?' Aria raised her voice, pushing past the paparazzo and using her body as a makeshift shield.

'Hey, I never got closer than six feet. Just trying to earn a living, lady. It's nothing personal. He's some fancy Italian billionaire, you'd think he'd be used to this.'

With a shrug, the pap turned and jogged away down the street, leaving Aria alone to deal with said fancy Italian billionaire, who was now really in difficulty. He pushed away from the tree, listing to one side as he tried and failed to gather himself. His eyes widened when she moved closer and grabbed his hand.

'Are you okay?' she asked, then instantly scolded herself. 'Sorry, that's a stupid question. You're clearly hyperventilating. Are you asthmatic?'

The man shook his head, somehow managing to look haughty and irritated by her babbling even as he fought to remain upright.

'Okay...maybe try to count out your breaths?' she urged him, using her hands to mimic the action of slow calm breaths in and out of her own chest. She felt rather helpless, her mind clutching at the few times she'd helped Priya through moments of anxiety. Assuming that was what this was. His breaths were coming sharp and shallow, even as he held her at arm's length, trying to get himself under control.

'Mr... Bacchetti, Nysio, was it? Let me help you.' She eyed him, wondering if he was too far gone to even register her words. But then his blue gaze met hers, the pleading look in them the first sign of vulnerability he'd shown. She was deeply relieved when he allowed her to take his hand, using his own fingers as tools to count out his breaths.

'Focus on your senses one at a time,' she said calmly. 'Look at my hand on yours, feel my touch, listen to my voice. Breathe.'

After a few minutes, his erratic breathing began to slow and Aria let out the breath she'd been holding herself, glad that he wasn't in danger of fainting on her. He was incredibly tall and even more broad and she wouldn't have had an easy time trying to break his fall. Now that he was out of danger, she should leave. Time was ticking and she still needed to track down Priya and figure out how on earth she was going to get home.

But when she made to take a step away, he surprised her by holding onto her hand. The heat of his skin seared into her, sending shivers up her wrist. She wanted to pull away, to keep some space between them, and yet she remained firmly in place.

'I'd just like some privacy for a moment. I have no wish to engage with any more of the New York press just yet.'

She frowned down at his hand, puzzled by something. 'Were you invited to the wedding today?'

'No. I'm here on business.'

'That paparazzo mentioned that you are someone important. A billionaire.' She narrowed her eyes on him. 'But I saw you watching all the drama from across the street. Then you waited around afterwards…why?'

She moved to step out of his embrace, but her dress had somehow got snagged on a low-hanging branch during their conversation and the resulting pull made her trip, falling sideways into him. He reached out to steady her, his hand coming in contact with her bare knee-cap. The touch made her entire body jolt, as though a current of electricity had passed from his strong fingers and into her skin.

Their eyes met and she gulped. That same angry vulnerability still burned in his deep blue eyes but the pupils were now wider, his nostrils flared slightly and she was pretty sure that his chest was rising and falling a little faster than it had been seconds before. Was she imagining it or was he flexing his fingers ever so slightly, tightening that grip and watching her reaction?

He inhaled sharply, still not fully recovered. 'I told you, I'm here on business. I stopped to make a call…but then I saw everyone leave and you remained. I intended to come to your rescue. Not the other way around.'

Against her will, Aria found herself smiling, a shaky laugh escaping her chest at the utterly ridiculous turn this day had taken. 'Just your friendly neighbourhood superhero in a pink bridesmaid dress.'

'Bridesmaid?' He frowned.

'Did you not see the bride who just ran off down the street? My best friend. Well, possibly my ex-best friend now that she's abandoned me here.' She rolled her eyes. 'Quite inconvenient when I'm supposed to be on a flight back to London in less than three hours and all of my things are in her apartment.'

'So I was right, you *were* in need of assistance.'

'I suppose so.' She shrugged, tensing at just how uncomfortable it felt to admit that. To admit that she needed help. For so long now she had made a point of ensuring she got by just fine on her own, not relying on anyone else. Things were just easier that way. Safer.

He was quiet for a moment, his eyes assessing her with a shrewd intensity that made her squirm a little. Her chest flushed, her skin felt slightly fizzy and, well…it was quite embarrassing, the effect this man was having on her.

'I happen to be on my way to the airport. Let me help you.'

'You would offer to help a stranger, just like that?' She raised a brow, wondering if his hyperventilation had made him dizzy or something. He was clearly someone important. He would have far more pressing things to do.

'What's your name?' he asked, his posture rapidly straightening back to what it had been twenty minutes before. When he had stood below her, gazing up at her with such imperious purpose. 'You know mine, and you can do and internet search on me too if that helps. Once I know yours, surely that would make us acquaintances at the very least?'

'It's Aria,' she breathed, trying not to be distracted by the effect that this man's proximity seemed to be having on her. The sodden material of her dress was still warm from his body heat, but cold where the loose skirt blew against her thighs. She felt off balance and completely unsure of herself. Perhaps that was why she remained silent and actually considered his offer for a moment before shaking her head.

'I have no passport or ticket, and my luggage is all locked in my friend's apartment. Even if you could somehow help me resolve all of that and get me on a later flight, it would mean I wouldn't arrive in London until much later and I have to get to work.'

'I have never encountered a problem that I couldn't solve.'

His words almost made her laugh, but then

she looked at his expression and realised he was completely serious. He had the power to get her on a flight, even without her documents. She had gone out of her way to fly to New York at the last minute, knowing that her friend was in a worrying situation and possibly in need of rescue. Maybe for once she could put her own situation first and accept when someone appeared to be doing the same for her.

'You came to my rescue here today, Aria. I'm simply asking for an opportunity to return the favour. I cannot restore your lost friend or your lost luggage, but I can get you home to London before dawn. That is a promise.'

CHAPTER TWO

FROM THE MOMENT she decided to throw caution to the wind and nod her agreement, things moved quickly. Aria felt butterflies fill her stomach as Nysio's car moved smoothly through the rain-soaked streets of Manhattan and then out of the city. Her mind raced, guilt mingling with anger as she tried to tell herself that she was doing the right thing, putting herself first for once. She had tried calling back the number Priya had contacted her on but had got no answer, not even a voicemail.

She was so deep in thought that she didn't realise that they were driving away from the main international airport until the car slowed down to enter a private airfield.

Security waved them through and her handsome rescuer brought the car to a stop alongside a sleek white jet. Aria felt her jaw sag. 'When you said you could get me on a flight...

I was thinking you had contacts in one of the airlines.'

'Is this a problem?' He frowned.

'It's a private jet.' She stared out at the sleek unmarked aircraft, watching as a small crew descended the steps to greet them. 'Do you seriously own your own aeroplane?'

A weak laugh escaped her lips and for a moment she thought she might be on the verge of hysterics as he stepped out of the car and walked around to the passenger side.

Was she actually about to accept a ride from a billionaire on a private jet? Her original flight had been the cheapest seat she could afford on a standard jetliner, where the seats were cramped on her hips and she almost always ended up sitting next to someone falling asleep on her shoulder or loudly munching on cheesy snacks.

'I could try to get you on a standard flight if you prefer. I couldn't guarantee the same timeframe or ease, but if the thought of being contained with me for the next eight hours is an issue...'

'It's not you,' she said quickly. 'I don't usually accept help from anyone, never mind a complete stranger in the street.'

'A trait we share, it seems.' His jaw ticced. 'But your kindness today was...unexpectedly

easy to accept. I'd very much like the chance
to repay you.'

His low response surprised her with its honesty and the reminder of the intimacy of the
moment they'd shared on the street. She had
witnessed his private panic and seen how unsettled he was by needing assistance. Maybe
it was that common ground that made her step
out of the car and close the door behind her
with finality, her decision made.

His hand gently gripped her elbow as she
stood in the chilled evening air. The crew made
quick work of bustling them on board and a
grey-haired man appeared, introducing himself
simply as Gianluca. Her details were taken in
a calm, efficient manner that made her wonder
if this kind of situation was a common occur-
rence. They would be waiting for a short time
for travel documentation and other red tape to
be dealt with, but she was assured it would
be sorted with minimal fuss. Evidently, when
stranded in a foreign country, it paid to have
wealthy connections.

It was strange to hear her host addressed as
Signor Bacchetti, and Aria watched as he was
called to the head of the craft to speak privately with the pilot, leaving her sitting alone
down the opposite end of the enormous air-

craft. Now that they were on board, would he expect her to go and sit somewhere quietly? She could usually small-talk anyone's ears off but this guy…didn't seem like the chatty type. She fiddled with the small gold pendant she wore on a chain around her neck, an old birthday gift from Priya. Fidget jewellery, her friend had called it. Aptly named, the solid gold letter A spun within a series of circles and made for a helpful tool when she just needed something to do with her hands.

Nysio was intense and brooding in a way that made every nerve ending on her body tingle with awareness. For a moment earlier, she'd been sure he was about to kiss her and the thought had made her panic, pushing him away. But then he'd made it clear that it was only gratitude that had him holding onto her so tightly and she'd felt…disappointed. Ridiculous, really, she wasn't a teenager…so why couldn't she stop wondering about what it might have been like? She inhaled a deep breath, trying to shake off the shiver that instantly travelled down her spine.

As a child, Aria had often been told by her parents and older sisters to stop bouncing on the sofa. Or tapping her feet, or chatting non-stop about the various aspects of her school day that wouldn't seem to stop swirling around in her mind. One would think that as she grew up that kind of energy excess would have waned, but it had not. It had simply morphed into an internal restlessness that proved just as frustrating to manage. She'd been in her mid-twenties when a doctor had suggested ADHD as the root cause for her struggles.

Maybe it was simply the adrenaline of the day, but Nysio Bacchetti's presence seemed to reinvoke the echoes of the kind of heated, needy sensations she'd hoped never to feel again. She prided herself on always remaining in control during the pitiful amount of dating she'd done over the past decade. She was a social creature by nature and had always enjoyed the excitement of meeting new people. But when it came to romantic entanglements, she played it safe, never getting in over her head. She had given her own foolish romantic heart away to Theo as a naïve twenty-year-old, and that experience had left scars deeper than she could have ever imagined.

She was so focused on taming her own swirling thoughts that she hardly noticed Nysio's return. He lowered his tall frame easily into the seat directly opposite, his attention engrossed in a loose sheaf of papers that he'd spread out from a slim folder. He sighed and plucked a pair of sleek, black-framed eyeglasses from his inner pocket to begin reading, a fact that should not have made him look any sexier than he already did. But when he slowly licked one finger and flipped over a page with one strong hand... Aria's traitorous mouth let out an audible sound of appreciation.

He looked up instantly, because of course he'd heard it. He was sitting directly in front of her. One dark brow quirked in question and Aria felt as though the heat of a thousand spotlights had zoned in upon her.

'Was that a groan?' he asked, placing his papers down to give her his full attention.

'No...well, yes, but not for the reason you're thinking.'

'Oh? What reason might that be?' His lips quirked at the corners and she was pretty sure he found her awkwardness to be immensely amusing. She glanced away, silently praying that he would turn back to his papers as she felt a definite flush travel along her chest and up towards her cheeks. Her redhead's colouring was usually one of her favourite things about herself, but not today. Not when every X-rated thought she had around this man was so brutally obvious. If she had any doubt that he might not see the effect his presence had on her, he confirmed it when she looked back to find him still staring.

'You are even more beautiful when you're embarrassed,' he said softly. So softly she almost thought she'd misheard him for a moment. He hadn't given any indication of being attracted to her so far, had he?

But she couldn't deny that all of a sudden the air felt charged between them, just as it had on the street outside the courthouse. His eyes darkened, his gaze falling to where she could feel her embarrassment had now heated the skin on her neck and chest to a rosy hue.

'You are blushing, Aria,' he remarked, his voice a low murmur, his attention unwaveringly rapt upon her. 'Have I made you uncomfortable?'

'No, of course not,' she said quickly, shaking her head as she rose to her feet. Ever the gentleman, he stood too, his frame broad and looming above her now that she had removed her heels. Before she could embarrass herself any further she mumbled something nonsensical about needing to freshen up, but really she just needed to step away. To gather her composure and remind herself that accepting this man's offer of rescue was just a means to an end and not some wild beginning.

She walked further down towards the end of the cabin where she could see a large master bedroom through an open doorway. She debated going inside but chickened out at the last moment, turning into the doorway on her left instead. She gazed longingly at the full-sized waterfall shower inside the spacious bathroom; this place was more like a penthouse apartment in the sky and most certainly an upgrade from the commercial flight she'd been booked on. If only she had her luggage with her, she would have jumped straight into the shower to wash off the city mud and grime.

Longing overtook her as she stared in the mirror at her dirty reflection. Her dress was no longer damp from the rain, but it felt sticky on her skin. She took a washcloth and ran it under some cold water, dabbing it against the sides of her neck and along her chest. A sigh escaped her lips as the cool conditioned air hit her skin and she felt a little relief. Sadly there was absolutely nothing to be done to save her sheer stockings so she decided that disposing of them and going bare-legged was better than being covered in mud splatters.

She reached under her dress, unhooking the

clip of her garter belt, and rolled off one ruined stocking with a sigh before changing to the other. She had just gripped the material at her thigh when she heard a gruff inhalation of breath behind her. When she looked up towards the doorway, she found she was no longer alone.

Nysio had simply intended to follow Aria to apologise for his forward behaviour, instead he'd ended up transfixed in the bathroom doorway, frozen in place as she slowly rolled her stocking down one leg.

Unaware of his presence, she'd pulled her skirt up higher, baring just a hint of the pink-and-black-printed lingerie she wore beneath, and he'd forgotten to breathe for a moment. The resulting gulp of air he'd taken in had alerted her to his presence, making her jump with fright.

Nysio instantly raised his hands and took a step backwards. The door had been ajar, but still…his reaction had not been one of innocence and the last thing he wanted was for her to fear him. As if he were a creep standing outside a window trying to catch a look at his obsession. He was *not* obsessed. He was perhaps a little more interested in her than he had been in any woman in a very long time…but he was not past the point of his own self-control.

'Apologies, I didn't mean to alarm you.'

'Top tip? Maybe don't stand silently in a doorway if you don't want to alarm the person inside. I could have been nude.'

He pushed away the instant image his mind tried to conjure at that statement and nodded, schooling his expression to one of remorse. 'I came in here to apologise for unsettling you and now it seems I have only succeeded in making things worse.'

He was seriously losing control of himself. First the impulsive trip across the Atlantic and now acquiring an unexpected detour and a guest on the journey home. He had already made the decision to leave New York immediately once he'd discovered his half-brothers were far too occupied in their own personal matrimonial race to bother threatening him. But for some reason leaving *her*, leaving Aria alone… It had felt wrong. Now here they were, having been alone on this jet less than half an hour, and he was already thinking of ways to get her even more undressed than she was right now.

'You didn't make me uncomfortable. It's just that…well, you keep looking at me like *that*.'

She gestured towards him. 'The smouldering eyes and the unblinking stare. I'm honestly trying to figure out if you're planning to murder me once we're up in the air, or…'

He felt irritation break the surface of his control. Was she truly this oblivious to the effect she was having on him? Did she not feel it too? 'I'm not planning to murder you.'

'Well, that's a relief, I suppose.' She let out a small laugh, but her mouth remained tight and her eyes lowered as though she couldn't quite look at him.

'Is this a game that you play?' Nysio took a step into the room, unable to resist the invisible thread that seemed to be pulling him towards her. 'The pale pink dress in the rain, the refusal to behave like a damsel in distress…now this *blushing*. Is it real?'

'It's my natural skin tone. Of course it's real.' She took a step towards him, her little dimpled chin tilting up stubbornly as she pressed a single pink-painted fingertip in the centre of his chest. 'How dare you? You are the one who insisted on helping me, remember? If anyone was a damsel in distress today, it was you.'

The reminder of his vulnerable moment was like a shock of cold water over his libido. He'd thought he'd got the anxiety attacks under control, but then again, he hadn't travelled this far from his home in an entire decade. As though she felt his shift in mood she took a step closer, her features softening.

'I'm sorry, I didn't mean for that to come out that way. I promise that I really don't see your moment earlier as weak. You just…seem to have got under my skin.'

He'd got under her skin? Nysio fought the urge to laugh. Good, that made two of them now, at least. He realised that if he'd been an honourable man he would have walked away. He would have removed himself to the furthest end of the jet and maintained maximum distance until she was safely deposited on English soil. He inhaled a breath then fought the urge to groan as her delicious scent filled his lungs, scrambling his senses all over again. Her sweet perfume was everywhere. He couldn't get away from it.

'I…don't wear perfume.'

Nysio looked up and met her questioning gaze, realising he must have spoken the words aloud. 'Your soap, maybe?'

'Maybe you should hold your nose, then. But don't forget to breathe.' She nibbled on her lower lip, the ghost of a smile playing upon her lips. She was trying not to laugh at him.

Rather than feeling affronted at her reaction, Nysio smiled, feeling his usual serious veneer slip completely as he realised the utter absurdity of their situation. He'd set out to play the chivalrous hero with this woman and she continued to surprise him at every turn. Was he truly annoyed at her for smelling good? He felt his own chest rumble with laughter and was shocked at the sensation of the mirth in his chest loosening the tightness there. Was his life really so devoid of humour that verbally sparring with this fireball of a woman could affect him so?

Lyrical laughter hummed from between her berry-coloured lips and Nysio found himself mesmerised by how the light made her lips shimmer. Would she taste as good as she smelled? Desire trickled along his spine, tracing down below his belt. He was suddenly very aware of their proximity and decided he needed to put some space between them pretty soon or she'd notice the thickly growing evidence of his sudden shift in mood.

Their eyes met and once again he found himself absolutely transfixed by their depth and gravity. By the time he realised he was moving closer to her, it was too late. Her balance swayed and all of a sudden she was in his arms, her lips seeking his. He allowed himself one maddening caress of his lips on hers, drinking her in like a drowning man before he forced himself to pull back for a moment.

'I didn't offer to take you on my jet for this purpose,' he said heavily, staring into her eyes and trying to ignore the fact that their bodies were still completely fused together. 'I don't want you to feel like this is what I expect from you…like some kind of twisted payment for your airfare. I can still arrange for you to get another flight.'

He waited a moment, studying the reaction on her face as it slowly changed from lust to disappointment. He wasn't lying, of course he would let her walk off this plane if that was what she wanted. He could be a gentleman, despite the teenager's libido that had seemed to overtake him ever since he'd set eyes on her. He would get her on the next flight home…

'But I don't want to do that,' he admitted, shocking himself with his own honesty.

'You don't?'

'Do you?' he asked, his eyes not leaving hers. She seemed to consider her options for a moment. He took in the stubborn set of her jaw and tried to ignore the sensation of something shifting into place within him like a car engine roaring to life when she finally looked him in the eyes and bit her lower lip softly.

'I want to stay here,' she confessed in a whisper. 'With you.'

He ran a finger along her lower lip, tracing his hands along her jaw before gripping the soft skin at the sides of her neck. Her pupils dilated just as he knew they would.

At the first subtle nod of her chin, he closed the space between them. He bent his head, following the line of her jaw with kisses, trying and failing not to groan a little as he inhaled some more of the warm scent she wore. It was sharper in the hollow where her neck met her shoulder and she shivered when he pressed his lips there, lingering for just a moment.

He leaned back against the wall and used the front of her gown to pull her to him, perching her side-saddle against his thigh. This position evened out their height difference a little, giving him much more freedom of movement.

'Do you feel this same energy, humming in your veins…demanding a release?' he growled.

He heard the arousal in her voice as she murmured yes, and he could sense her body telling him what he wanted to hear. But still, some part of him wanted her to leave, wanted her to run away from him and whatever madness this was between them. He didn't quite trust it, the seemingly effortless flow of mutual attraction that pulsated between them. Perhaps for her it was simply the aftermath of the adrenaline of the day and the chaos that came with it. He wanted to test it out, he wanted more time.

'I want to be the one to give you that release,' he said, inhaling her sweet berry scent and feeling it scorch his lungs. 'Do you want me to kiss you again, Aria?'

CHAPTER THREE

'YES.'

The word was the barest whisper on Aria's lips before Nysio's mouth was reclaiming hers and she felt him press her backwards, caging her in against the wall. They kissed for what felt like hours, his mouth devouring hers with expert precision, and she was lost…completely lost to whatever madness this was that had taken hold of them both.

She wanted it never to end. She wanted him to consume her whole and put out whatever needy fire he had ignited within her.

She'd never felt arousal quite like this, not even the handful of times she had actually enjoyed sex in her life. She had always been too self-aware, too inside her own head.

Why wasn't she overthinking everything right now? She had never felt this way before, as if she were in a freefall of pleasure, on the brink of madness. And madness was the only way she could accurately describe the feverish sensation taking over her body. It was reckless and heady and a part of her felt as if she needed to revel in every second, just in case it was all taken away again. Her throat was dry, her pulse racing as he began a hot trail of kisses from her ear down her neck. One strong hand cupped the side of her jaw while the other traced along the side of her breast and down the curves of her waist and hips before settling with a firm squeeze upon her behind.

'From the moment I first saw you, I wanted to do this,' he murmured against her skin, pulling back for a split second to stare into her eyes in the dim light. Searching...

She exhaled, a soft moan escaping her lips as she felt his grip tighten, his fingers pressing into her flesh through the fabric of her gown. His lips resumed their kisses and licks along her collarbone, his clever fingertips found and pinched her nipples through the flimsy pink material.

'You are so honest in your reactions...even when you hide, your face tells me what you're feeling.'

His sensuously accented words circled around her, increasing the impression that she had entered into some kind of trance. Perhaps this was not reality at all. The sensation of his touch and the soft gravelly whisper of his words seemed to melt into one, drawing her deeper and deeper into this intoxicating battle that she never ever wanted to leave. Everything melted away replaced only by him.

'What am I thinking right now?' she asked softly, splaying her hands through his long thick curls and feeling a strange comfort in the silky warmth she found there.

'You're wondering if I'm just a cocky bastard or if I'm actually going to make you come, right here.'

'Oh. Can you…do that?' she stuttered, hardly believing how brazen she felt.

'The question is not *if* I can give you pleasure,' he replied with a wicked tilt of an eyebrow. 'It's about where you'd like me to start.'

The look in his eyes made her pulse quicken and a fine point of heat began to throb between her thighs. She thought of all the clever things she might say, to seem sophisticated and seductive, but came up short. She had never been good with silence, it made her twitchy, but this silence was heavy and laden with dark twirling tension. She smiled nervously, pressing her lips together. She should lay the ground rules, she thought. She should say…something.

But no sooner had she opened her mouth to speak than his head was descending for another punishing kiss.

Aria thought she had been kissed before. She had a vague recollection of how the act was supposed to feel…but this was something else entirely. Her body felt as if it had been plugged into a stream of vibrant electric energy, the kind that fuelled euphoric fever dreams. She felt his strong hands against the sides of her neck, anchoring her and angling her jaw upward as he took everything she offered.

This was a kiss of pure domination, something that should make her run a mile considering her track record with wealthy domineering males. Why wasn't she running? Why did the thought of this kiss ending make her want to dig her nails into this man's arms and refuse to let him go?

It seemed he had been holding back before. This kiss was brutal, a magnificent storm of perfectly aimed sensuality that utterly ruined her for any kiss that might come after. He was all hard male, brawn and beauty as he caged her against the marble-topped vanity until she leaned against the mirror. The cold glass dug into her back, the slight hit of pain only seeming to heighten the wicked pleasure of his mouth as he began to trail hot, suckling kisses down her neck.

'Do you realise how long I have been waiting to get you alone?' he murmured against her skin, his hands greedily savouring the full weight of both of her breasts through her dress.

'We only met for the first time about an hour or so ago.'

'Believe me, I know,' was his only answer, as if that were explanation enough. Then he continued his ministrations, sliding the square neckline of her gown low enough to tease one breast free from her bra.

His fervent murmur of approval chased away the ever-present layer of anxiety that lay in wait, threatening to ruin the mood with the slightest hint of rejection. She wasn't insecure about her plus-size body, but her performance in bed…well, there were still some scars there that had never quite healed. A small voice in her mind told her to be careful, to slow down a bit.

Sex wasn't easy for her, not with the way her mind liked to wander and delve into everything. It was probably the reason why she had never reached orgasm in any way other than by herself, in the dark alone at night. Every time she'd got close to being assertive in the past, to asking for what she'd wanted, that voice in the back of her mind had chimed in. The one that spoke in Theo's voice and told her that she would never be good enough in bed, that she should be grateful for what she was given. But the thought of scaring Nysio into stopping made her clutch his shoulders tighter.

She gasped as Nysio leaned forward, pressing the evidence of his arousal against her stomach. The difference in their heights was probably close to a full foot, so he compensated by taking her hand and placing it right...there.

The action was so hot, and the evidence so undeniably large...she almost begged him to just take her right there on the floor. He clearly was thinking something similar as his eyes scanned the immediate area, his breath coming in harsh bursts. He swiped the surface of the vanity clear with one hand, sending small plastic bottles of soaps and lotions crashing to the floor. Aria eyed the surface incredulously, sure it looked pretty solid, but she was short. He couldn't actually expect her to hoist herself up there while he...no way.

'Let me help.' He didn't await an answer, gripping her hips with his big hands and lifting her with ease as though she were a dainty doll and not a fully grown woman. Who knew she had a strength kink? But wow…that was hot!

For a split second he simply looked at her, his expression so reverent and hungry it created a pulse of longing between her legs. But then he was standing right between her thighs and his mouth was everywhere. He really liked her breasts, that much was certain. But he also liked her neck…and her lips. She knew this because he growled it, in between kisses. He was quite vocal in his lust, a fact that made her relax more and more with each new touch and caress. But when he began to pull the hem of her skirt even further up her thighs, she stiffened.

'Wait,' she breathed. 'I don't know if I can…'

He stopped instantly, holding himself so that even though their bodies were still pressed together, the gap between their faces gave an illusion of space. A rough laugh escaped his lips and he shook his head, as though he too could feel the absurdity of the moment. At how quickly things were flying beyond their control. She braced herself, waiting for his regret. But instead of coming to his senses and pulling away, he tucked one errant strand of hair from her face and slid it behind her ear.

The air between them was silent and still

for a moment as they just stared at one another. She could still feel the press of his muscular abdomen holding her thighs open and the clear shape of an unmistakeable erection. All that separated them was the thin fabric of his clothes, her dress and bra, and the barest slip of her matching strawberry-printed high-waist thong. The urge to tilt her hips upwards, to move against that hard heat, was almost unbearable. He felt it too, she realised as he began to adjust his position then froze, a low hiss escaping his lips.

'I don't have any protection.'

'Oh.' She breathed, sheepish that she hadn't actually thought of that herself. 'I'm on birth control. I haven't been with anyone in a long time, but I know I'm safe in that regard too.'

'Me too.' He spoke the words against her skin, his hands stroking up and down her spread thighs. 'It's been years since I've even gone on a date.'

Aria paused, wondering if that kind of dry spell was enough to explain their complete loss of control. Was he using her simply as a convenient way to break his long drought? Did she care? Wasn't she using him too, in her own way? Maybe it was enough that they were both using each other in this moment. Maybe that was what made it even more magical.

'All I know is I can't seem to stop touching you. I don't want to,' he growled.

'Then don't,' she whispered, writhing in his arms as he continued his path of sensual destruction downwards, his tongue and hands invoking an equal amount of pleasure.

Madness indeed. Stunned laughter threatened to escape her lips as Aria met his gaze and realised that she was going to do it, she was actually going to make love with this handsome stranger on his private jet.

'I can feel your heart beating under my tongue,' he said softly, lacing each word with such dark promise it made her skin prickle and her insides melt. 'Right here.'

She thought of all of the reasons why she shouldn't be doing this, why she should have run far away from such a scandalous proposition from a stranger. But she had spent so long holding in every impulse she had, playing the good girl, and look where it had got her.

Perhaps just once, instead of feeling guilty about her own life choices, she could simply do what she wanted to do. And right now…she knew exactly what she wanted.

She lowered the straps of her dress and bra

down and pushed the garments down below her breasts.

'It's been a while for me,' he warned. 'I don't know if I can be gentle.'

'I won't break,' she promised, her skin sizzling with excitement at his words. But it was the truth. It was the one secret fantasy she'd always harboured but never managed to realise, to be taken fast and hard this way. No preamble, no time for her brain to overthink anything.

Her words only seemed to spur him on further and he pulled the gown up towards her waist in one rough tug. Thank goodness it was a stretch material or he might have ripped straight through it. Actually…that might have been kind of hot too.

She gasped and accidentally released a small giggle as his fingers slid along the sensitive skin of her hips and he moved her thong aside. Their eyes met and for a moment she worried she'd ruined the mood, but then he smiled and let out the sexiest husky male laugh before claiming her lips once more.

It was the kiss of a man on the edge of his control. Their eyes locked for a moment and it took her a couple of beats to understand that he was waiting for something from her. His eyes searched her face and for a moment she thought she caught a glimmer of the mere mortal underneath his all-powerful façade. But just as quickly, it was gone again and he was back in control.

At the first touch of his erection against her molten heat, Nysio almost lost his sanity entirely. Or what had remained of his sanity from the moment he'd met this beguiling woman. She'd exploded into his orderly life like a monsoon, hot and wet, just as she was right now. He moved, unable to stop himself from plunging fully inside her in one torturously slow slide.

She hissed just a little, her body initially resisting the intrusion and he searched her face, confusion and concern threatening to call a halt to his entry.

'I'm okay,' she murmured. 'You're just…big, that's all.'

Flattery was always welcome, but her discomfort was evident in the taut set of her mouth and the tightness around her eyes. He should have prepared her more—he had barely been in here two minutes before he'd plunged himself inside her like an impatient teenager.

'Just need you to…' She breathed out slowly, biting her lower lip as he slid back and forth the barest few millimetres. 'Yes…like that.'

'I should have gone slower,' he said regretfully, resisting the urge to speed up, to deepen their intimate contact.

'No, this is perfect. Everything is perfect.'

Their matching groans of pleasure were perfectly in sync, just as their bodies were as he kept a tight hold of one gloriously rounded thigh and increased his rhythm. Her skin was butter soft and begging to be licked, but he'd make time for that later. He'd make love to her slowly next time. He wouldn't let her out of his bed until she was crying with pleasure, exhausted and muttering his name like a curse. He wanted to ruin this woman for all others. He wanted to claim her.

The thought made him pause, his breath heaving in his chest like an approaching battle drum. And yet he was past the point of heeding his own intuition to walk far away from this beguiling beauty with her sharp tongue and vibrant spirit. He thrust again, taking her faster and harder, as she breathlessly urged him on. Far be it from him to deny a lady's demands. But the tempo crashed through what remained of his futile control, bringing his own release closer with a powerful sizzle of electricity downwards along his spine. He was close, too close.

He paused for a moment, closing his eyes in a frantic attempt to delay the powerful onslaught of his own pleasure. This feeling…this riotous lack of finesse…he hadn't felt so undone since his youth. Even then, he'd had the good manners to ensure his partner had reached their own pleasure before he dived into seeking his own. But he was already inside her and she was writhing against him, urging him to recommence the harsh rhythm of moments before. She met his eyes, vulnerable and unsure. He leaned down, taking her mouth deep and hard to reassure her that he was still very much okay, too okay truthfully. With one hand, he widened her thighs and pressed his thumb against her centre.

'Is this what you need?' he asked, cupping her jaw with his free hand as he continued to rub slow circles on her swollen bud.

Long lashes fluttered open, pinning him with vibrant green eyes that were dreamy and out of focus. She moved her hips, guiding him to increase the pace of his fingers against her flesh, and as she became more breathless he felt his own excitement build.

'Yes, that's it, come for me,' he demanded, trying to hold himself still in an effort to slow down, but as she began to writhe against him he didn't stand a chance. Nysio let out a guttural curse, his body helpless not to move, to *take*. Two more thrusts were all it took before his release came crashing over him like a tidal wave he had no hope of holding off.

Reality descended swiftly, and he looked at her, searching her face. 'I didn't intend for that to happen. Not until you'd been satisfied.'

She avoided his eyes, sliding her hands down to cover where she was still spread open and bared to him. 'It's okay. I've never been able to…get there.'

'Not even from your own touch?'

Her cheeks bloomed an even deeper shade of pink. 'That's different.'

'It's not.' He saw her visibly shrink from him, her discomfort and unfamiliarity with his concern evident. She moved to straighten herself further but Nysio kept his weight right where it was, his hand centring gently on her chest.

Her eyes widened and for a moment he was fully sure she would push him away. She looked uncertain and deflated as she tried to relax back. Tension filled her shoulders and the lines of her mouth.

'You were close…weren't you?' he murmured, sliding his hand to cup her over the wet, strawberry-patterned silk. 'You were so close to losing it for me.'

'Really, you don't need to do this.' She gasped as his finger slid along the inside of her thigh.

He leaned down, resuming his torture of her breasts. He took his time, glorying in each light moan that escaped her lips as he savoured her with his tongue as though he wanted to devour her whole. In a way, he supposed that he did. He felt wild and untamed, so completely far apart from the beacon of control he had fought hard to become in the past ten years. He was ready to lose himself all over again in this woman, and to hell with the consequences.

He looked down at her, gripping one of her wrists and holding it high above her head to keep her where he wanted her. This was good, he reminded himself, control was good. With his other hand, he tested her wetness with his index finger, watching her face until her eyes darkened and he knew he'd found exactly the right spot. Her breathing deepened and her hips moved ever so slightly.

'I want to taste you while I make you come.' He breathed the words against her ear, punctuating the final syllable with a soft nip of his teeth against her skin.

'No.' She stiffened a little, still circling those delicious curves against him. 'No tongue. Just…just touch me, please.'

'Whatever you need,' he murmured again, shocking himself with how calm he sounded in light of the battle drum pounding within his chest as he got down to his knees before her.

A second digit joined the first and he kept up the same steady rhythm until she began thrusting back against him. He found his rhythm, spreading her even wider. When he hit a certain point inside her, what little control she had shown unravelled completely. Her hands gripped his hair as she writhed and let out the most delicious breathy moans he had ever heard. He felt her tightening around his knuckles and he remembered the force of his own release, remembered spilling himself inside her and claiming her as his own.

The thought made him pause. She was not his, she was just a stranger who had come crashing into his life. But then she looked at him, cheeks rosy in the afterglow of her pleasure, and he realised with a stunning bolt of clarity that he needed to make love to this woman again. More than he had ever needed anything before.

He was fully hard and ready to go again almost instantly and he cursed low in his throat. This didn't happen to him. This couldn't happen. This woman was a walking liability and he had done something with her that he never normally did. He had acted on impulse. But as he stared at her he felt something else coil tight within him. Something darker and needier than lust, and infinitely more dangerous. He wanted her, the kind of want he usually reserved for the things he kept out of public view. His hobbies and passions.

The things that were his very own.

He moved backwards as though burned, averting his eyes and doing up his trousers as she slid the skirt of her dress back down into place.

This was a problem.

CHAPTER FOUR

IT TOOK A few moments for Aria's soul to return to her body. But when it did, she realised with swift clarity that he was not feeling quite so relaxed as she was. Her arms were still clasped around his shoulders and she could feel that he was very much still engaged in the moment but...something felt off.

'You said you never come with someone else.'

'I usually don't,' she breathed, her heartbeat still loud in her ears.

'I've never been so turned on; just watching you lose it for me has me ready and wanting you all over again...and again...' His voice was a gruff groan, his words more of an accusation than a lover's whisper. But the look in his eyes was what almost undid her completely. He looked...tortured. Over her? How on earth was this even possible?

Her thoughts jumbled over one another in an effort for first place and as a result she said nothing at all.

'We should take a moment,' he said. 'Slow down.'

'Of course.' The polite response escaped her lips on a reflex, followed by silence as she watched him put as much space between them as humanly possible. He stood with his back against the black tile wall on the opposite side of the opulent bathroom, his chest still heaving and his eyes pinning her in place. Like a man who had just come to his senses, her inner voice, still sounding like Theo, sneered.

She exhaled a slow shuddering breath and tried to get her wobbling emotions under control. She had long ago vowed never to shed a tear over anyone who could walk away from her so easily.

No, whatever emotion this was had to be something to do with the massive release her body had just experienced. The aftershocks of which had barely even subsided and her body was throwing a tantrum, demanding more of him. What on earth was she doing?

Mortified, she began to pull up her bra and the material of her dress to cover her still bare breasts. The silk fabric had already been tight, but now that it was damp from both the rain and the kisses he had dragged over her skin it hiked her breasts up into a lurid cleavage. Her nipples were still hard from where they had been practically devoured, and she inhaled sharply as the dress caught on one jutting peak.

'What are you doing?'

Aria looked up, to find herself pinned by a dark gaze as he watched her.

'Getting dressed, obviously.' She choked out the words, praying she could hold herself together just long enough to get far away from this too-small bathroom with all of its mirrored surfaces. She turned away to face the small vanity, but there he was reflected in the glass. Everywhere she looked, she saw him.

The realisation that they hadn't even taken off yet made her stomach sink even further. They still had an entire transatlantic flight ahead of them. As far as impulsive actions went, this one was pretty spectacular. 'I didn't intend for this to happen.'

'I never said you did,' he said.

'Well, I just needed to clarify that. Considering you're looking at me like…like you regret everything we just did.'

He watched her for a moment, then he bridged the space between them, hooked one finger under her chin and tilted her face up until she met his gaze. 'You could not be further from the truth. Do you regret it?'

'We literally just met,' she muttered. 'It's all a bit overwhelming.'

'That's not what I asked.' His eyes darkened even further, impossible considering they were already glittering obsidian. 'I just had the best orgasm of my life and yet I immediately want to take you again.'

She was pretty sure she felt her jaw drop, her mind stunned to silence. But what else was a girl to think when a guy made her see stars and then tried to put as much space between them as humanly possible right after they had just...*you know*. She shivered, hearing the way he pronounced orgasm repeating over and over in her mind. The way he looked at her, the way he made her feel... She had always thought people simply lied when they said sex could be addictive. For her, it had always been a chore, a performance. But now...now she finally understood.

'I don't regret it, Nysio.' She reached out and touched her hand to his shoulder, still clad in his shirt. 'And actually that was the best orgasm I've ever had too.' She simply wanted to show him that she understood, that she could see this loss of control was affecting him just as much as it had affected her. But her words and her touch seemed to be the only spark needed to reignite the madness once more.

This time when his lips claimed hers, there was no restraint whatsoever. It was as though the man who had devoured her moments before had been a mere appetiser to this. His mouth was cruel, demanding and utterly sinful as his tongue tangled with her own. His hands gripped her waist tight, holding her in place as though he feared that she might try to leave.

Yet somehow she knew that if she did call a stop to this right now, he would. Whatever this was between them was not about either of them holding more power or manipulating one another or seeking a reward, this was pure primal lust as she had never dreamed of experiencing. It had been pretty easy not to date much when she had never really enjoyed things in the bedroom.

Strong fingers moved up her ribcage and his hips pressed harder against her, spreading her wide again, his eyes seeking hers, questioning...

'You said you want me again...then have me,' she said boldly, determined to wring out every last drop of pleasure from this night. Because she knew that tomorrow would come and she would be back to the cold, harsh reality of the life that awaited her in London. Was it really so bad to choose to live in a dream for a little while?

'The plane will take off soon. But first, I think you wanted to get freshened up?' He began taking off her dress and she let him, feeling it pool around her feet. He tried to unclasp her bra, but she had to help him.

'The clasp is quite tricky. I still haven't quite mastered that part of the sewing process.'

'You made this?' His brows rose. 'You're a fashion designer?'

'Well... I want to be.' She smiled, wondering why it felt more intimate to be having this conversation than any of the other interactions they'd had during this wild evening. But before she could stop herself, she was launching into telling this half naked stranger about her plan to pitch a boutique plus-size lingerie line at her team evaluation meeting tomorrow. How it was a long shot, but she had to try. She knew the fashion buying and marketing business like the back of her hand and now she had practical experience in the design and manufacturing processes too. She'd done all the numbers and she knew it would work, she just needed them to believe it too.

If he was surprised or bored by her enthusiasm, he didn't show it. He studied the strawberry-print silk bra in his hands, analysing the stitching and boning she'd agonised over during her final examinations, and placed it down carefully on the vanity as though it were something precious.

'If you are this passionate about everything you do, I expect them to jump at the chance to keep your vison and skill on their team. I know I would. Passionate people are few and far between in my world. It's mostly about routine and consistency...and money.'

'I'm ADHD, so excitement is fuel for me. Boredom and routine are rather painful.' He nodded with apparent understanding, a strange look entering his eyes for a moment. Why was she oversharing so much? She cursed herself, wishing he would just start kissing her again so she'd stop talking.

'We are very different people, aren't we? But perhaps that's why I can't get enough of you. You're like an injection of pure energy. I haven't felt this alive in a long time.'

His shirt joined her dress on the floor, then the rest of his clothing. He walked them backwards towards the rainfall shower, reaching out to touch a button that set hot water cascading down. His eyes met hers, his hips rocking that hardness against her for a moment. 'Once we're up in the air, I'm determined to get you into an actual bed and not let you back out for a very long time.'

Aria woke with a jolt, her sleep-fogged brain struggling to make sense of the current time and place. The bed was empty and the white sheets were a tangle around her body, a crude reminder of last night's erotic efforts. She held her breath, craning her neck to listen for any sounds of life beyond the bedroom door.

No Nysio, she registered, refusing to note her own disappointment at that fact.

They'd landed on the tarmac in London before dawn and what had been meant to be a goodbye kiss had ended up with both of them falling back into bed for yet another quick round of mutually explosive lovemaking. She must have fallen asleep again afterwards...and he'd left. She covered her face with her hands. She was trapped in here, naked, and whoever was outside the door was likely fully aware of that fact. The memory of her gown and underwear sliding over her body and abandoned on the bathroom floor was branded in her mind, sending a fresh wave of goosebumps along her sensitive skin.

She flopped back against the luxury mattress, as soft as air. She refused to feel ashamed of last night, when it had been so life-changing for her. She'd known what this was.

But had he really just left her without so much as a goodbye?

No, she was not going to lie here and feel even a tiny bit sorry for herself. With a deep fortifying breath, she stood up and wrapped the white sheet around her torso like a toga. The wall of mirrors in the luxurious master cabin mocked her with her own ridiculous reflection, showing panda eyes and the utterly destroyed remnants of her bridesmaid chignon.

Memories assailed her mind from the night before, tightening up every muscle in her body with a mixture of embarrassment and astonishment that it had all been real. She had truly been seduced and pleasured by a billionaire on his private jet while they flew across the Atlantic. She would not regret it, not when her body felt so deliciously satisfied and loose from pleasure. They were both adults, after all.

He had said he didn't make a habit of picking up women, but he'd admitted he was under pressure. Tensions were high and she had been a…convenient outlet.

He hadn't kidnapped her onto his jet, she'd walked on of her own free will. She'd given into temptation all over again. More than once. She closed her eyes, exhaling a shaky breath as she tried to get a handle on herself.

She hadn't known her body could work that way. She'd always known her previous experiences in the bedroom had been uniquely bad and unlucky, but wow. The flight had lasted eight hours and she was pretty sure he had made it his mission to make her lose count of the amount of times they'd made love before she fell asleep in an orgasm-drunk haze.

Was it even a one-night stand if they had crossed time zones?

Considering she had to slip back into her gown from the day before, she decided to forgo using the lavish shower again. Her pendant necklace had disappeared from her neck and she tried to keep calm as a quick search of the cabin came up empty. Another look in the mirror confirmed that she looked exactly like a woman who was about to make the walk of shame off a luxury jetliner. Not exactly a sentence she'd ever thought that she would use in her lifetime.

There was only one staff member still on board when she exited the bedroom and walked gingerly along the central cabin in her bare feet. A quick search along the floor produced her shoes and little clutch bag. But it was okay— a quick look at the time on one of the screens showed that it was still early enough for her to make it back to her basement apartment in Richmond and quickly change into something before her usual commute into the city.

But when she exited the jet, the morning light momentarily blinding her as she stepped out into the chilly English air, it was to find a dark car coming to a stop mere feet away on the tarmac with the object of her thoughts behind the wheel. She inwardly cringed at the situation, pasting on a much too bright smile as Nysio stepped out and turned up the collar of his tan jacket against the harsh breeze.

'I apologise for leaving without explanation, but you needed some sleep and my presence was needed to resolve a small dispute with the customs officer.' He moved to the rear of the luxury car and produced something from the back seat. 'I was hoping to return with this before you woke up.'

In his hands was a suitcase. But not just any suitcase. It was her very own neon-pink one, easily recognised by a large blue ink splash from where her pen had exploded mid-flight at some point during her last travelling spree. She felt her jaw go slack, a handful of questions crowding her mind all at once.

'How did you get it from Priya's apartment?'

'I have people.' He shrugged.

Aria took in his calm expression and admitted he didn't look quite like the rueful morning-after guy on the run she'd expected. But that didn't mean anything, did it? She didn't want it to mean anything, and she had told him exactly as much last night. So then why did it make her heart jump a little when he looked at her?

'I'll wait here while you shower and change.'

Aria took the bag, silently walking back towards the bathroom, her heart beating fast in her throat. There had been absolutely no need for him to go to such lengths to retrieve her things. But as she opened up her suitcase and spied the black high-waisted trousers and baby-blue blouse she'd chosen specifically for her presentation she felt her throat tighten with emotion.

She was just tired, she told herself. Tired and nervous about work and still recovering from the whirlwind of the day before... And the night.

She took the quickest shower known to man, dried off and dressed, staring at her reflection in the mirror sternly. She would not keep thinking about the night. With a light slick of matte red lipstick, and a quick kiss blown in the bathroom mirror, where she absolutely did not gaze longingly at a certain countertop while her cheeks blushed, she was ready.

When she emerged once more, taking the steps slowly in her kitten heels, Nysio was still leaning against the bonnet of his car. He opened his mouth as though to speak, then closed it again and, for the first time since they'd laid eyes on one another the day before, an awkward silence fell between them.

Nysio had expected someone who worked in fashion to dress well, perhaps one of those businesswoman shift dresses with office-appropriate heels. Of course this woman would turn office fashion into something better suited to the pages of a risqué magazine. Or perhaps there was nothing risqué at all and he was simply looking at her through the new lens of knowing exactly what hid beneath the satin layer of her delicate blue blouse. He wondered if she still wore the strawberry bra beneath and his mouth quite literally watered. *Dannazione*, his thoughts had a mind of their own around this woman.

She looked unsure. He knew he should say something—he should tell her that last night had been wonderful, because it had. He should tell her that when he had awoken after losing count of how many times they'd made love he had been busy making plans to see if he could stay in London for a few days. He wondered how she might react to the proposition. But before he could say any of that, Aria was the first one to speak.

'Okay… This is the part I was dreading.' She avoided looking directly at him while shuffling through her purse.

'What part might that be?'

'The whole awkward morning-after part.' She finally looked at him, her smile a little too bright and not quite meeting her eyes. 'So I'm going to make it really easy, I've already asked the crew to call me a cab.'

'Easier for whom?' he heard himself say.

'For both of us, I suppose. This way, there are no empty promises or small talk. I get to my presentation on time and you get to go back to your fancy billionaire life after taking this… detour.'

'You think I see you as a detour?'

'No. I just mean that it was all very unexpected and neither of us was in the market for anything more than one night. Right?'

He allowed silence to follow her question, his mind stumbling over the threads of his own intentions. He remembered holding her in his arms, in between the copious rounds of sex they'd shared. They had laughed, they had spoken of trivial things, never getting too deep. But still, he'd got the impression that she had been hurt badly in the past. She'd told him that she didn't date much now as a result, that she was focused on her career. But if he asked to see her again, would she assume that he was offering her more than just a casual affair?

Once upon a time, he had been supremely sure that one day he would settle down and marry, continue the family line. But now... now that he knew his position, his very identity as the Bacchetti heir, was built upon nothing but lies...he knew that he would never put his own child in that position. The darkness of his thoughts must have shown on his face, he realised with chagrin as he looked up to find Aria still studiously avoiding his gaze.

'Well...' Aria shuffled awkwardly on one foot. 'Thank you for everything.'

'You're thanking me as though I have provided you with a service of some sort.'

'A very efficient service, if that helps?' Her laugh jarred his nerves with how false it sounded. Gone was the confident, honest siren from the night before and in her place was someone he had no idea how to read. Those walls he had had to work so hard to dismantle the night before had clearly sprung right back with extra reinforcements.

'I'm confused… Have I misread something?' she asked, just as a second chauffeur-driven car slid up beside his own. His ever-efficient crew had been all too eager to help his guest, it seemed. The driver stepped out and called her by name, taking the suitcase from her hands and stowing it efficiently in the rear before holding open the passenger door.

'My presentation starts in less than an hour, so I asked the crew to call me a car. I assumed that you would have things to do.'

'You *assumed* that I make a habit of sleeping with women and disposing of them like trash. I promised to deliver you to your interview.' He gestured to the car behind him. 'And that's what I plan to do.'

'Oh… That's very kind of you. But completely unnecessary. I came to your aid back in

Manhattan, and you felt obligated to repay me. Last night was amazing, but there's no need for either of us to make out that it was more than a pleasant distraction for us both.'

Her words should be giving him comfort, but instead he found himself holding back from lifting her back up onto the jet... He scowled, watching as she turned to him and for a moment he feared she might reach out and shake his hand. He had never experienced this before; any entanglements he'd had in the past had been ended by him. Was that why this felt so uncomfortable? Was he so privileged and entitled that he was balking at the idea of her being the one to walk away? Perhaps he needed to ensure that he was the one in control.

He took her hand, meeting her eyes in the golden morning light. 'What if I asked you to come and join me in Florence for another weekend of...pleasant distraction?'

'Why would you do that?'

'Why not?' He shrugged. 'It could be fun.'

She seemed to deflate at his answer. 'I could really like you, Nysio, if I let myself. But I've learned that when I like someone, I really like them and, well... It tends to just get me hurt. I don't think either of us is prepared for this to get any more complicated than it already is.'

With a final kiss on his cheek, she got into the car and was gone. Nysio scowled again, not quite pitiful enough to watch the car's departure across the tarmac. The jet's interior was a quiet welcome, Gianluca appearing predictably at his side to ask if he'd made a decision on their flight plans.

'Get us slotted in for the next departure time to Florence,' he said, aware that his tone was far surlier than necessary.

'Back to our usual routine this week, then?' the older man asked.

Nysio nodded, feeling far less satisfaction with the idea of returning to his old normal than he'd ever thought possible.

CHAPTER FIVE

ARIA'S PRESENTATION WENT without a hitch as she knew it would. Fake it till you make it was her motto and by the time she was walking out of the conference room full of executives she was filled with hope that this was actually going to happen for her. The strange aches and twinges in her body had lasted for a few days, a crude reminder of her wild night of passion every time her mind tried to convince her it had all been a mirage. She spent the rest of the next two weeks working extra hard on her usual projects as her team awaited the results of their evaluation.

Of all of the outcomes she'd expected, it wasn't to walk into work the following Monday morning to find that their entire clothing department had been made redundant. Moving to an online-only model had been one of the biggest terms thrown around. She'd cleared out her desk in a daze and found herself at home sitting on her couch by lunchtime after a tearful goodbye.

News of the shocking lay-offs had made global news and, one week later, flowers had appeared on her doorstep accompanied by a small box containing a golden necklace that almost exactly matched the one she had misplaced on the jet. It was not the same one, she could tell, because this one was clearly infinitely more expensive.

The note read:

My offer still stands. If you find yourself with time for another adventure, the city of Florence will await you.
  Just call.
  N

Aria ran a finger over the embossed gold lettering from the boutique florist. There was no way he could have known that she'd just been made redundant, was there? No way he could have known how badly she'd needed some kind of pick-me-up as she'd found herself sitting around in her own self-pity. In the past three weeks, she had thought of that mile-high night of passion more times than she could count. She had wondered where he was, wondered if he was thinking of her too. But she also remembered how Nysio had admired her underwear design and listened to her plans, how he'd seemed to truly believe she had a chance at success. He'd called her passionate.

She didn't feel especially passionate now, in the face of her defeat. But still she found herself digging out her plans and projections, an entirely new and infinitely riskier plan beginning to form in her mind. She was unemployed for the first time in a decade, but she had her nest egg from the redundancy pay-out, which had been generous in lieu of a long notice period, and she could get a bank loan for the rest. Starting up a plus-size lingerie line alone as an entrepreneur was a ridiculous idea…wasn't it?

She smiled, picking up another sample design and feeling her brain hum with plans and ideas. She had spent so long trying to rein in her high-energy mind and not make mistakes. She'd finished her textile degree against the odds, she'd worked hard and advanced through her job all while sacrificing her love of travel and spontaneity. She had often dreamed of taking some time to wander, to fall back in love with the world and come up with a way to forge her own path on her own terms. Maybe it was time for her to stop hiding away her passion and let herself run wild with it?

As she stared at the vibrant flowers on her coffee table and opened up the envelope containing a number for a premier flight operator and details of a prepaid ticket, she felt tempted to be spontaneous once again.

Nysio cursed and slammed the lid of his computer down. His concentration had been atrocious over the past month and he'd just made yet another careless error in his projections, resulting in an unprecedented loss of capital that would have brought most investment firms to their knees. Luckily for him, he was not most investment firms and his unusual business practices meant that his reserves ran deep. Of course, this was now the third day this week that he'd made a mistake and his accountant had even called to ask what on earth was happening.

And what exactly *was* happening? he asked himself, pushing his chair back from the antique mahogany desk in an effort to not give in to the impulse to hurl something against the wall. He had not been himself ever since that impulsive trip across the Atlantic. It was the only possible explanation. The return journey, specifically…

An image of flame-coloured hair and strawberry-scented skin filled his mind as though it had been waiting for the right moment to assault his senses. His stomach clenched, his fists tightening against the rush of arousal that always accompanied thoughts of her.

Her.

That single pronoun was how he'd been subconsciously referring to the woman who had occupied a space in his mind for almost a month now, as though the use of her name might cement his obsession any further.

Not an obsession, he corrected himself. He was not under some kind of thrall. Their night of passion on the jet had just knocked him off kilter, that was all. It had been far too long since he'd been with a woman, it was only natural that he wouldn't be satisfied from just the scant few hours he'd had her. Especially when she had walked away from his offer so easily.

He had returned to Florence and thrown himself right back into his usual punishing work routine of eighteen-hour days spread across the various global stock markets. He'd got used to keeping odd hours, filling any downtime by working up a sweat in his gym or swimming length after length in the heated pool in the solarium. When he was physically and mentally exhausted enough, he eventually slept. But never for long enough and never quite as deeply as he had on that jet…

He stared out at the view from his window, wondering why memories of that one night felt like a drug. Other than that, the only time he broke his rigid routine was the bi-monthly weekend he set aside to spend visiting his parents in Sardinia. A visit he had postponed in the aftermath of last month's revelations about the identity of his biological father. His mother had called numerous times and he was pretty sure they knew he was avoiding them. But the alternative was actually facing the reality that his father was not his father and his parents had lied to him for his whole life.

He had always adored the blissful silence and solitude of the *palazzo* in the evenings after all the staff had returned to their homes in the city, but these past weeks he'd found it made him feel tense and on edge, as though he were waiting for something. Since his return, he had struggled to fall back into the few leisurely pursuits he allowed himself like reading or cataloguing his vast wine collection. He had tried, countless times, but his eyes would blur along the lines of text, his mind wandering to other, more X-rated thoughts.

As a result, the insomnia that he'd thought he had fully cured himself of with his exercise regime had now returned with a force that left him restless and wandering the halls.

One night in particular, he'd found himself in the pantry of the kitchens searching the shelves for jars of preserved sweet berries and jams, opening each one and inhaling deep, only to curse and move on to the next, furiously seeking the one particular scent that his memory was unable to fully recall.

Nysio hadn't even realised he had left his office and begun pacing the halls until he found himself staring up at the vaulted ceiling of the ancient family gallery that ran the length of the ground floor along the vast east wing. He scowled up at the painted cherubs and imperious gods and goddesses, feeling their judgemental gazes bear down upon him. This had always been Arturo Bacchetti's favourite place in the *palazzo*, before his parents had retired to the vineyard in Sardinia. The gallery was a place that Nysio actively avoided, now that the more historic parts of the estate were occasionally opened to the public.

Their family's status was one that was

earned, not only by their vast fortune and collections of priceless art, but by their position as the city's most prolific charitable benefactors. Their presence at their historic Florentine *palazzo* provided year-round tourism for the locale. They provided patronage for local artists and funded most community efforts. Many of the other noble family names had died out, but the Bacchettis had remained. And perhaps that had been a cushy position a hundred years ago and more, when the Bacchetti family had been far more numerous and able to widely delegate.

Now, there was only Nysio.

He ran a finger along a glass case that housed a four-hundred-year-old golden throne, wondering if smashing some priceless and irreplaceable Bacchetti heirloom might jolt him out of this wretched stagnation he'd fallen into.

As if on cue, Gianluca appeared in the entryway, as though he had sensed Nysio's temptation to destroy a part of his beloved estate.

'You're not normally out of your office at this time,' the other man said, dropping a box full of freshly printed tourist guides onto the floor beside the door before surveying him with concern.

'I may as well be here.' Nysio sighed, looking at his watch to find it was only early afternoon.

'The markets are not my friend today. I decided it was best for all of us if I took a step away.'

Gianluca frowned. 'That's not like you. Are you ill?'

'I'm fine,' Nysio snapped. He was fine, he would be fine. Eventually... This feeling, it reminded him of the first few months after his father's Parkinson's diagnosis, after he had vowed to fully accept his role as Arturo's heir. To perform his birth-given duty, even if it suffocated him. He had been restless, fresh out of a short-lived post-university period of debauchery and rebellion. But what was his excuse now?

Surely spending less than twelve hours with the most alluring woman he had ever encountered was not enough to completely change his personality? It was ridiculous and infuriating and he would not tolerate it. He made a few enquiries about the day-to-day running of the estate, happy to distract himself with Gianluca's entertaining tales from the city before he turned to head back to work. As he moved through the *palazzo*, he internally readied himself to prove to himself that he was above such distractions, only to have the other man appear behind him in his office, jolting him from his thoughts.

'Nysio, I wasn't going to say anything...but,

do you remember your *guest* that we deposited in London a month ago?'

Nysio froze, his body turning around in slow motion as though pulled by an invisible string. 'What of her?'

'She's in Florence.' The older man met his eyes. 'She called at the estate foundation office in town yesterday, and made a donation for the exact same price of her flight.'

Nysio felt frozen in place. 'She's still here?'

Gianluca nodded. 'At least, she was when I checked earlier today. But her return flight is tomorrow.'

Nysio fought the urge to roar with frustration. She had been here for a whole day already without him knowing. He had been within walking distance of the object of his frustrations... But what did it mean? Surely if she had come to accept his proposition, she'd have travelled here to the *palazzo*. She would have come to him. He felt his chest tighten even more, some uncontrollable vibration of energy that seemed to rise from his stomach upwards, but he somehow kept his body completely still.

'Thank you for telling me, Gianluca.'

The other man's eyes widened. 'That's it?'

'Was there anything else you needed to discuss? I have work to do.' Nysio sat down behind his desk with barely constrained energy humming through his veins, the computer screen blurring in front of his eyes as his mind turned this new information over and over. On impulse, he pulled a small object from his pocket, turning the small golden letter A over and over in its miniature circle. The pendant had been broken from being crushed under someone's foot before he'd found it under the bed on his flight home from London.

He'd repaired it, but decided to send her a new one once he'd seen the news of her company's harsh lay-offs. He hadn't banked on the fact that every time he held it, he remembered seeing it dangling from Aria's neck as she straddled him, leaning over so he could suckle on her...

Gianluca's voice intruded on his thoughts. 'All I'm saying is, perhaps the lady wished for you to know that she was here. If she didn't, she wouldn't have left this note.'

Nysio's gaze snapped back up. 'What note?'

Gianluca smiled knowingly. 'It must be at least five years since I've seen you showing any kind of interest in a woman.'

Nysio narrowed his eyes, his look clearly conveying his inability to take a joke on the subject because the other man quickly pulled up a screen on his tablet computer and laid it on the desk. 'It was only given to me today.'

Nysio only half listened, his attention fully taken up by the few lines of communication thanking him for the ticket. She had not contacted him immediately after he had sent the necklace, the flowers and plane ticket. So he had accepted that she was serious about not continuing their entanglement any further. He had never been the type of guy to force his attentions on anyone, most especially on someone who had been clear that they were not interested in more. At least, she had *seemed* sure she was not interested in more…but the fact that her note was clearly headed with the name of the hotel she was staying in said quite a different story. He smiled broadly, inhaling a deep breath, and felt something loosen within his chest.

'Clear my meetings for tomorrow, Gianluca. Actually, clear them for the whole weekend.'

'Where are you going?'

'To be spontaneous,' he called back over his shoulder, striding out of his office and in search of the nearest car as fast as his legs would take him.

Aria was thoroughly enchanted by Florence.

For two glorious days, she had ambled

along narrow cobbled streets flanked by elegant Renaissance palaces, marble basilicas and world-class art museums brimming with iconic paintings and sculptures. It was quite a culture shock, travelling from her traffic-clogged London suburb to this small city with its extraordinary art and architectural masterpieces at every turn. It was quite possibly the most beautiful city she had ever visited.

But all the while she had found herself looking over her shoulder, hyperaware of her surroundings and wondering if she would turn to find a familiar pair of sensual dark blue eyes watching her.

There had been no need for her to leave the note at Nysio's foundation along with her donation, and yet she had not been able to stop herself. She'd told herself that she just needed to let Nysio know that she had used his ticket, and only because the flight had been the best option available at the last minute.

Perhaps she had also come here with a small hope that he might seek her out. But the idea of outright contacting him and accepting his arrogant offer to fly over to him, like a paid and packaged gift for his entertainment…she just couldn't bring herself to do it.

Still, she now knew by the disappointment

churning in her gut that she had very obviously hoped to see him again. It was her last night in the city and her small suitcase was packed and ready to leave for the airport back to London tomorrow. She was excited to get started on her plans. Her parents had been less than happy with her news when she'd shared her plans to start up her own line of plus-size lingerie. They'd sermonised on job security and the risks of start-ups. Her mother had made the predictable comment that she was *thirty-one*, as though that was a reason in itself to avoid following her dreams.

All of these thoughts seemed to compound into one giant splitting headache as her eyes fell upon the single cocktail dress she'd left hanging in the wardrobe. The midnight-blue mini was a custom piece from an exciting plus-size designer that she'd acquired for the store more than a year ago but never found the occasion to wear. With its full-length sleeves and deep plunging neckline, it was the kind of outfit that one wore out on a hot date, not down for dinner at her table for one before taking an early night alone…but then again, Aria had never been the type of girl to follow the rules, had she?

Feeling a spurt of energy, she showered and took some time to dry her hair in soft waves around her face, adding red lipstick and some smoky eye make-up. Simple black lingerie and stockings ensured she felt smoothed and supported and as she gazed upon the final result in the bathroom mirror, she smiled. The fabric of the dress sparkled like a night sky, the material clinging to her curves like a dream.

It might be overkill for a night dining alone, but if there was one thing that could be said about Aria Dane it was that she bounced back, every time. This weekend had been exactly what she needed to clear her head before she had a meeting with her bank next week to discuss her business plans. Her redundancy money was enough to get started, but not enough if things took off as she really expected them to. She wanted to be prepared.

By the time she was seated in the hotel's extravagant fine dining restaurant, she was feeling quite elated. The waiter had just delivered her drink order and she was perusing the menu when she felt the hairs on the back of her neck tingle.

With her wine glass halfway to her lips, she looked up to find the grey-haired maître d' hovering by her side with an unusually flustered air. 'Is everything okay?' she asked the man, noticing the slight sheen of sweat on his brow.

'Signora Dane, I have been asked to extend an invitation to you from a most important patron of the hotel…to a private dinner in the penthouse.'

'An invitation from whom?' she asked, thinking he must have approached the wrong guest, but then she looked behind her and felt her breath catch.

The important patron in question leaned against the archway of the restaurant entrance, his brooding gaze and broad silhouette unmistakeable in the golden light. Nysio was here… he had come to seek her out. Blood pounded in her ears and she could have sworn that every nerve ending on her body jumped to attention.

But his invitation to a *private* dinner made her pause. She might have come here with the intention of seeing him again but she had not been lying when she'd made it clear that she was not in the market for any further secret rendezvous. She had made a promise to herself that she would not be another wealthy man's secret lover, ever again. Even if said lover had given her the most pleasure she had ever known in her life.

The maître d' still awaited her response and Aria straightened her shoulders, determined not to lose her composure. 'You can tell Signor Bacchetti that I am flattered by his offer to dine privately, but I am going to have to politely decline. He is quite welcome to join me here at *my* table, however.'

'Signor Bacchetti does not dine with the other guests,' the man replied, clearly stunned at the audacity of her response.

'Well, it will be a novel experience for us both, then.' She took a tiny sip of wine, trying not to react at the sudden nausea it caused as it mixed with her swirling nerves.

The man disappeared from view and it took all of Aria's control not to crane her neck to look back. After a couple of minutes she gave in and felt her entire body react at the sight of Nysio making his way across the restaurant floor, his gaze filled with intent. He had told her that he shied away from the attention his name got him here in Florence, but she hadn't truly understood what he'd meant until now. The waitstaff around him bowed their heads in deference, a shocked hush carrying across the restaurant as though he were a celebrity or royalty…or both.

Frantically trying to get her erratic heartbeat under control, Aria remained frozen in her seat until he was but a few steps away, then realised she should probably stand up to greet him. The restaurant was full and it seemed as though every eye was upon them when he finally reached her.

'*Buonasera*, Aria.' His lips curved up ever so slightly on one side and she suddenly had another flashback to that night on the jet.

'I thought you didn't dine with other guests,' she said breathlessly, powerless against the shiver that coursed through her when he leaned in and laid a customary kiss on each of her cheeks. He lingered on the second cheek, his breath fanning over her ear as he paused there for the briefest moment.

'I usually prefer to dine away from prying eyes, yes. But I think I can tolerate it…in the right company.' His voice was smooth as silk as he let his eyes wander down over her body for the briefest moment, but it was enough to set her pulse racing all over again. This man was a menace to her composure, an absolute menace.

'Has no one ever told you it is considered rude to refuse a dinner invitation from the owner of the establishment?' he said silkily as he helped her back into her chair before sliding into the seat across from her.

'You…*own* this place?' She whistled low, looking round at the ornate vaulted ceilings and priceless art that lined the walls. 'I knew you were wealthy, but clearly you undersold it. I planned to buy you dinner, to thank you for rescuing me in Manhattan, but now I'm wondering if we should split the bill.' She laughed.

'You are now here as my guest. There will be no splitting the bill.' He uttered the phrase with distaste, as though she had deeply offended him, gesturing to the waitstaff nearby to come and take their order. 'If I had known you were planning to accept my offer, I would have ensured no expense was spared. For now, an upgrade to the penthouse will suffice.'

'Okay, hold on.' Aria sat up straight, feeling her irritation rise. 'You're rich, I get it. But I didn't come here to be given a free ride on the luxury billionaire train.'

'Why did you come, then?'

'I came to see Florence and I can pay for my own room, Nysio.'

'You can. But I'd like to show you my Florence, if you'll let me?'

If she'd thought his accent while speaking English was sexy, his voice as he spoke rapid-fire Italian almost set her aflame. She could do little more than sit and stare as he conversed personally with the chef, gesturing with his hands and pausing to translate and enquire in English about her individual preferences for food. When she explained that she didn't eat a lot of meat, he ensured that an array of tasting platters was brought out, each dish gourmet and more utterly divine than the last.

Occasionally, he seemed uncomfortable when other diners stared or spoke in hushed whispers, but mostly the meal passed in pleasant conversation as she talked about her recent entrance into unemployment. She attempted to sound relaxed, but he still frowned at her words.

'I'm sorry.'

'Thanks. I'm okay, though. I actually took some of your advice.'

'My advice?'

'I've always dreamed of starting up my own lingerie line, but I was comfortable in my job and I told myself I could never do it. But then you told me about how you incorporated your talents into your family business and made it your own…well, I found that quite inspiring.'

As the last of their desserts were cleared away, the air between them had become tense and fraught with countless words it seemed neither of them were quite brave enough to say first. He surprised her by taking her arm and guiding her through the lobby of the hotel where it opened out onto a private courtyard.

The sky was rapidly darkening to dusk, making the building glow amber, and tiny golden lamps accented the sprawling fountain in the centre.

'I think Florence has ruined me for all other cities.' She sighed with pleasure.

'Sometimes it feels like that,' he murmured, seemingly mulling over something in his mind as he paced away from her to inspect a statue in their periphery. When he spoke again, his eyes were more focused. 'The necklace suits you.'

Trying not to raise a brow at his odd manner, she smiled, her hand instantly moving to the golden pendant resting on her collarbone. 'It was very kind of you to send it. You didn't have to replace it.'

'I felt it was only fair, considering it was my fault the last one was lost.'

Aria's breath caught as she took in the heat in his eyes and knew that he too was remembering the events from that night. His eyes did not waver from hers. His hand dropped to his side in a clenched fist as though he was trying not to touch her again. Or was she imagining that?

'I didn't see the note you sent until this evening. You didn't respond to my gifts, you told me to stay away. I told you that I would not pursue you and I am a man of my word. But if I had known you were here…'

'You would have rushed straight to me?' She laughed, then paused, realising he was completely serious.

'Without a second thought. Still, it was not soon enough.' The last word escaped his mouth on a breath and again his hand rose, this time making contact with her skin as he gently grazed the side of her elbow. 'Aria, I am going to ask you one question and one question only before I do something that I've wanted to do from the moment I walked through that door this evening.'

Aria's chest tightened, her skin tingling with awareness as she saw the dark promise in his eyes. 'What question?'

'Did you really come here to explore the city...' he moved closer, his voice a low purr near her ear '...or did you come to me?'

Breath exited her chest on a shudder as she fought to contain the visceral reaction that she was beginning to realise always came from having him near. He was a magnetic force, determined to pull her off course every time their paths crossed.

'Because if you came to me... I have already been robbed of the forty-eight hours you've been wandering this city alone, when you could have spent them in my bed.'

'I realised once I was here that I came because I wanted more. But only on my terms. I want you to be *my* entertainment for the weekend, Signor Bacchetti,' she said with a wicked smile. 'I had planned to fly back tomorrow, but I might be persuaded to extend my trip a day or two for the right reasons.'

'What reasons might they be?'

His words were whispered huskily against her ear, while his hands finally gripped her waist, warming her skin through the thin material of her dress. She swallowed hard, planning to respond with something clever and sensual, something to let him know that she was the one calling the shots here...but then his lips touched the sensitive skin of her neck and she instantly seemed to lose the ability to form a coherent sentence.

'You want me to act as your personal tour guide?' he murmured against her skin. 'I will show you everything this city has to offer... You want to be wined and dined in the best restaurants and bought gifts from the finest boutiques? Tell me and I'll make it happen.'

She paused, pulling back to look into his eyes. 'Nysio... I told you already, I don't want you to buy me things. You're all the entertainment I need...that is, if you wanted to...'

Understanding dawned and his eyes darkened even further, his lips finally claiming hers in a scorching kiss. His hands fisted into her hair, his lips and tongue laying claim to her with a passion she had only ever felt in his arms. But if she'd thought that the kisses they had shared on the jet had been illicit and hungry, this one took her breath away.

CHAPTER SIX

HE HAD HOPED his mind had exaggerated the memory of having this woman in his arms, but now he knew that the opposite was true. She seemed to not be aware of the connection between him and her friend's new husband, Eros Theodorou, and for a moment a part of him almost wished that she did. That she had stumbled upon his secret and he was forced to keep her here, to ensure that there hadn't been any more leaks. Maybe then he could explain why he felt such possessiveness over her.

She moaned under his kisses, pressing her gorgeous breasts up against him, and he realised that if he didn't get them somewhere private soon, he would be powerless not to take her on the nearest flat surface.

Reason and propriety won out and he guided her through the hotel lobby towards the private elevator that led up to the most exclusive suite in the hotel, the penthouse. Of course, the three minutes it took to get to the top provided him with just enough time to release one ample breast from the neckline of her dress and give it one thorough suck before he tucked it safely back from view of wandering eyes.

Did she know how much power she had over him? He should slow down, regain control and tell her his rules. The problem was…he had pretty much broken every rule he had from the moment he'd laid eyes on Aria Dane. He'd pursued her, he'd changed his plans, he'd ignored his work. He tried to stir some sense of remorse in himself, but found himself smiling instead.

This woman was like a single bright spark in the darkness. He couldn't look away. She caught his eye, an answering smile crossing her lips as she extended her arms to him, drawing him in closer. Holding him to her as though she feared he was about to disappear too.

Weakness overrode his common sense and he went with her easily, moulding his body against hers on the large four-poster bed that dominated the Royal Bacchetti suite. There would be rumours in the papers by tomorrow, no doubt. He hadn't dined with a beautiful woman in public since his days as a young man on the party scene. Back then, he'd always needed to be a few drinks in before he could loosen up enough to not feel the effect of others watching him. He was very careful what he drank now, for good reason. He had always found difficulty in moderating his use of anything that provided him with relief from his anxiety, from the burden of being a Bacchetti.

Joy, relaxation, happiness, these were all emotions that were in short supply in his world and yet one look on Aria's face and he saw all three. During dinner she had conversed with wild abandon, her emotions open, her face unguarded and absolutely fascinating. He could study her for hours, just as he had once studied ancient tomes from his favourite poets or his favourite classic paintings. He had always been a lover of the arts and she was like a newly discovered fresco, rare and filled with untold meaning and fascination.

When she moved against him he didn't make any move to disguise his attraction, just as she didn't try to hide her own. Such honesty…it was as heady as any drug. She licked her lower lip and gazed up at him through hooded lashes, her cheeks pink as she moved against him. Her eyes widened when she came into contact with the unmistakeable hard ridge of his erection, but she made no move to retreat.

He sucked in a breath through his teeth and tightened his grip on her arm. The urge to pull her into the nearest bed was strong. He wondered how she might respond if he told her how he wanted to have his way with her... He felt unhinged, like some kind of depraved primal beast. He wanted her spread out like a sacrificial offering at an altar, laid bare for him.

But this was not the Middle Ages, he reminded himself as he fought to control his body's complete disregard for propriety. She was a person, not an item for him to take and ravish.

Accepting her proposition felt like the prelude to possibility. The possibility of something more. Suddenly the things that had felt so urgent no longer seemed so important. Not when she looked at him like *that*. As he undressed her and finally sank into her molten heat, he wondered if it would ever be enough.

Aria took her time showering after a second night spent in Nysio's arms. They had hardly left the ornate four-poster bed of the hotel's penthouse suite. The experience was only slightly marred by the steadily tightening knot of nausea and nerves that was building in her stomach as the afternoon progressed. She could only assume that such nerves had something to do with her handsome date for the evening, which was silly considering this wasn't a date at all but a peace offering.

One of the maids had brought up a glass of champagne and a bowl of strawberries for her to enjoy as she readied herself for a surprise date Nysio had organised for her last night in Florence. Fresh flowers had also been arranged on her dressing table, pink roses today rather than the usual simple arrangement of magnolias that were placed strategically throughout the hotel. All in all, it was a lovely way to spend the afternoon, she thought absent-mindedly as she dabbed blush onto her paler than usual cheeks. She took a moment, stepping out onto the balcony for a few deep breaths and willing the bubbling nausea to settle.

By the time Nysio returned from a quick trip to his office she thought she'd got it under control but one look at his face said otherwise.

'Are you feeling well?' he asked, his eyes roving up and down as he assessed her closely.

'Thank you, you look lovely too.' She quirked one brow, nerves making her spin in a silly little twirl. 'My dress? Oh, it's just something I dug out of the wardrobe.'

'You look pale.'

'I'm fine. Just some cramps.'

His brows rose slightly, but he seemed unperturbed. 'Do you need something? Aspirin, perhaps?'

Aria inwardly prayed for the ground to open and swallow her up. The man looked like a god in his designer suit and she was talking about *cramps*?

He touched her hand, stilling her thoughts as he waited for her eyes to meet his. 'You look beautiful, by the way. I probably should have said that first.'

'Thank you.' She felt the butterflies swoop and dance in her tummy all over again as he leaned down to lay a featherlight kiss upon her lips. 'I'm going to stop talking now, lest I start rambling about other bodily functions.'

'Let's not aim for the impossible.' He smirked, leading her outside where a sleek silver sports car lay in wait.

He wore a full tuxedo for the occasion, and she hadn't quite been ready for the visual onslaught of seeing him in formal dress. His hair, usually curled and unruly in its natural state, had been slicked back from his forehead in an effortlessly elegant style.

She found it hard to continue being annoyed with him when he was so obviously trying for her. She just wished she knew why. He had made it quite clear on the jet that night that he was comfortable in his workaholic bachelor lifestyle and she'd thought she had made her peace with that. They were polar opposites in most ways other than the bedroom, so really it was best not to get too attached. She could only assume that tonight was a peace offering of some sort before they parted ways. Her flight had been rebooked for tomorrow morning, her suitcase was neatly packed and her room already put to rights.

It was all very civilised really, she thought as she wiped what was most definitely *not* a tiny tear from the corner of her eye.

As they were served a five-course meal in Nysio's stunning town house in Florence by a world-class chef, she wrestled with the steadily rising discomfort in her gut. She hadn't felt any nerves on their first night together, or their second, so why was she feeling such unease now? Such was her digestive discomfort, she could barely manage a drop of wine and the sight of the pink-centred venison main course made her stomach heave a little.

'Is everything okay?' Nysio asked. His brow furrowed with concern when she stood abruptly from the table and walked to the open patio doors for some fresh air.

'I'm fine,' she assured him. 'Just a little warm.'

She was warm; she had been feeling over-heated all week, in fact. But just as she moved to suggest that perhaps Nysio should take her home, the bell rang from the foyer and the butler came in to announce that the evening's surprise entertainment had arrived.

The surprise turned out to be a private performance from a world-renowned opera singer and her accompanying Grammy-winning pianist husband. Nysio's town house was far from small considering it had its very own ballroom in which to enjoy this auditory extravaganza.

The lights had been dimmed, and candelabra lit, making the room seem to glow with atmosphere as the first strains of music floated through the air.

The private show was short, but breathtakingly beautiful, and Aria was stunned as she learned of the many countries in which the duo had performed together, and the names of the numerous members of royalty and governments and celebrities they had performed for made her eyebrows rise into her forehead.

Even though she had dressed the part, wearing a knee-length fifties-style black gown and elbow-length gloves, she still felt the pressure of having to appear cultured in the way that these people clearly were. She had not been raised in this world, a fact that she had no reason to hide but, hearing Nysio discuss the elite university he had apparently attended alongside the beautiful opera singer, she prayed that the conversation would not move onto her.

He left to see them outside and she found herself feeling a little dizzy so she located the nearest place to sit, which just so happened to be at the beautiful piano at the edge of the dance floor. It was an antique Steinway, the black enamel so beautifully preserved and polished that she could see her own reflection in the case. She sat down, dancing her fingers playfully across the keys with a flash of memory.

The song was one she'd learned by heart years before, but it seemed her fingers needed no further notice. She played the simple piece in full, a smile filling her lips as she finished on a perfect chord. She didn't notice she had an audience until she heard the slow clap from behind her.

'When did you learn how to play?' Nysio walked slowly into the room from where he'd perched against the doorway.

'My father refused to pay for lessons because he said I would only quit and it would be a waste of money, so I bought a keyboard and taught myself a few pieces when I was a teenager just to annoy him. I haven't played in years. I don't read music or anything fancy like that. I'm not actually trained.'

'You are full of surprises, Aria Dane.'

'I like to think so.' She gave a delicate curtsy, standing up from the instrument and swaying a little before she corrected herself. She still looked too pale, he thought as he moved to take her elbow and guide her out onto the terrace. She had barely eaten at dinner and there was something just a little off...

She moved to stand beside the stone balustrade, gazing out at their perfect view of the Duomo lit up in all its glory. He wondered if she liked it, if she was enjoying the evening. He'd thought that perhaps the champagne and flowers had been too much, but she hadn't said anything to the contrary.

'It's so beautiful,' she whispered.

'Yes,' Nysio agreed, watching the glitter of the skyline dance in her eyes. How fitting that this woman would be named for both the life force that filled his lungs and the most striking and poignant moment in any opera. As though she could be named anything less.

'How come you don't live here?' she asked, turning to look at him and startling a little to find his eyes already trained upon her.

'This place was a remnant of my old life. I have no need for it any more since I moved to the *palazzo*. I have rarely left the palace grounds in the past decade, ever since...'

'Since what?'

'My father became suddenly unwell soon after my graduation from university, and my mother was struggling to care for him and keep him from becoming prey for the media. He has Parkinson's and it is a difficult condition to live with, very unpredictable. He is a proud man, quite old school, and he wished to keep his illness private. I stepped in to take his place as the head of our family. So I don't have much need for a party house any more.'

'I beg to differ. This place is a wonderful space to entertain in. There is always a need to dance. To have fun. To enjoy occasions with friends.'

'I have no time for any of those things. Once I stepped into my father's place, I discovered issues with the finances and set about resolving them.'

'You suddenly became allergic to fun?'

'I suddenly realised how empty the party scene was. I decided to dedicate my energy to better things.'

'Like crashing stock markets and increasing profit flow? That kind of thing?'

Nysio smiled, against his will. Something that she was beginning to make him do with increasing frequency. 'You don't have any idea what my job is, do you?'

'How could I? You are a man of mystery. I know that you're pretty rich. That you're descended from some kind of blue-blooded Italian royalty.'

He steeled himself against the sting her words gave him and forced himself to smile. 'Hard to hide that with the whole palace situation though.'

'Then… Tell me something new about yourself. Share a secret.'

He looked away, busying himself by clearing away their glasses to a nearby side table. She couldn't know that so much of his world was built around secrets. Maybe it was the lack of stress in the past two days or maybe he'd uncharacteristically drunk too much wine with dinner after all, but Nysio felt something within him stir at her innocent request. A yearning that begged him to do just as she asked…to share his darkest secret. To lean on someone.

'Have I…said something wrong?'

She was frowning and he realised he hadn't spoken in a couple of minutes. He shook it off, closing the distance between them and claiming her lips in a soft exploratory kiss. Using the easy attraction between them to soothe away the prickly feelings this conversation had unearthed. She relaxed into him, giving back as good as she got, but when the kiss finished her eyes still held echoes of confusion. Nysio rubbed his thumb along the soft curve of her shoulder and felt an ache throb from somewhere deep in his chest.

'I like poetry,' he said finally.

Aria blinked, her mouth forming a small o for a split second until she grasped that he was in fact answering her earlier request. 'Are we talking limericks and haikus?'

'The dirtier the better.' He smirked, feeling his chest ease slightly at the smile that lit up her face. 'No, I actually took a few classes in university. I read every poem I could get my hands on. It consumed me for a semester or two.'

'Did you ever write any of your own?' She narrowed her gaze upon him, a Cheshire-cat smile taking over her face. 'Oh, my God, you did, didn't you? Can I hear one?'

'I may have written some terrible, brooding sonnets, yes. Ones which will never, ever see the light of day to avoid offending the art itself.'

'Please?'

He let out a wry laugh, remembering his youth and how he had once dreamed of joining the ranks of the writers and poets he admired. Without thinking, he began reciting the first refrain of the only one he could remember. On the surface it was a simple collection of words about a drunken man having an argument with the night sky, but to him it was filled with frustration and a longing for change.

When he'd finished, he cleared his throat, not quite able to look at her for fear of what emotions might be visible on her far too honest face. 'Have my literary talents rendered you speechless?' He laid his glass down on the nearby side table, leaning back and crossing his ankles to survey her. She had one hand on the balustrade, the other splayed across her chest as her eyes drifted open slowly.

'That was…hauntingly beautiful.'

'My professors certainly thought so; it was my one and only claim to fame as a creative writing student before my father made me switch to an economics major.' Nysio remembered how embarrassed he'd felt when his father had discovered his new hobby and had begun reminding him of his responsibilities. He'd felt ridiculous for even considering his brief dream of forging his own path when he'd been raised to perform his duty to the family name.

Being a Bacchetti was a privilege, that was what he had been taught from the moment he'd been old enough to speak. He enjoyed his work now and he was good at it, and that was more than most people ever got in their lifetimes.

He turned back to the woman before him, reaching out to touch her once again, remembering the words he'd planned to speak tonight before they had become sidetracked. But really, this kind of ease and intimacy was only more evidence that his instincts were right. That he was not ready to say goodbye to Aria Dane just yet.

Aria met his gaze so openly and he felt as if he could see every needy part of her, every salacious thought that she was entertaining about him. How could one woman affect him this way? How could one look ignite passion in him that he had never felt before?

She had been hurt by a wealthy man in the past, she had told him that much. It had made her hide away much the same way that Nysio had been hiding at the *palazzo*. Perhaps that was what he had seen in her? Perhaps that was why whatever this was between them felt like more than simple chemistry. There was nothing simple about it.

He couldn't offer her anything more than pleasure…he would never marry, never have children, that much he would not be swayed upon. But they didn't need to put a label on things. She had told him she believed in spontaneity, so maybe it was time that they acted a little spontaneous.

Aria could hardly believe how wonderful this trip to Florence had been. And Nysio…he was a dream. 'So…you live in a palace, you write poetry in your spare time, when you're not breaking the stock market, of course. What *can't* you do?'

'I'm just a man.'

'That word seems so utterly banal to describe someone who does the things that you do. And yet you hide yourself away in your stone fortress. Hiding your talents from the world, keeping it all to yourself. Why do you do that?'

He shrugged. 'Maybe I simply dislike people.'

'No… That's not it.' She took a step towards

him, analysing the furrow between his brows. 'There's something you're not telling me, isn't there?'

'Perhaps.'

'These things… You don't have to tell me about them if you're not comfortable. I won't dig, if you're worried.'

'Did I say I was worried?'

'There it is, that fragile ego.' She smiled good-naturedly. 'I just feel like someone needed to remind you of what the world actually sees. What your talents are, your value,' she said softly.

His eyes met hers and she inhaled a breath at the sudden intensity she saw there. He took her hands, stepping closer so that they almost stood chest to chest.

'Aria… I know that tonight is your last night here. But I brought you here…to this property to show you what might be if you reconsidered my offer from London.'

'Isn't that what we've been doing these past couple of days?'

'Yes, but I was thinking of a more regular set-up.'

She felt her stomach drop instantly. 'Please tell me you're not about to suggest that I become some kind of kept mistress.'

'That's a very outdated phrase. I was thinking more of two consenting adults who live separate lives but regularly enjoy each other's company.'

'You want to…date me?'

'I don't *date*.' He practically growled the word. 'I want to continue getting to know you, but I don't want to give you the wrong idea.'

'Oh, heaven forbid.' She laughed, moving away from him.

He held onto her wrist. 'I don't think this has run its course yet, do you?'

For a moment, Aria thought she'd heard him wrong. That she was simply grasping onto a wishful hope that he might actually want her, truly want her. But then she heard that word again: yet. Meaning that he thought this would run its course eventually. That even if she stayed for a while, it was inevitable that he would eventually tire of her.

'Do you feel fully satisfied?' he asked, his low rumble coming from just behind her right shoulder. Soft lips touched against the side of her neck and she felt her heart throb a little. She couldn't tell him the true reason why she needed to leave…not without risking something far more delicate than just her pride, something she didn't want to examine too closely.

She turned her head to find him standing directly behind her, his brow furrowed as he tried to read her face. He struggled with that sometimes, she realised. She recognised that often he needed to hear the exact words from her, plain and simple rather than relying on guessing games. She loved how plain and honest he was. She loved being here with him, talking with him…

If she gave more of herself to him on his terms, he had all but written down in ink that he would take it. Passion, sex… But nothing more. She knew with heartbreaking clarity that something more, a deeper connection, was what she truly wanted. Yes, the sex had been amazing, but the man she had come to know over the past forty-eight hours was infinitely more attractive to her. And infinitely more unattainable.

But was she really prepared to walk away from him completely? Would this be the single moment she looked back on in her old age and wished that she had done differently?

She had promised herself that she would never again be made to feel disposable by a man. Prolonging this affair was only prolonging the inevitable moment that he would break her heart, a heart that, if she was honest, was already falling headlong in love with him. The longer she stayed here, the more it would hurt when he walked away.

Her tortured thoughts seemed to be having an effect on the rest of her body as she felt another violent surge of nausea sweep over her like a wave. Determined not to show how unsettled she was by his offer, she turned from him and leaned on the balustrade to try to compose herself. When she seemed to sway forward slightly, Nysio was right there beside her in a flash.

'Be careful you don't hurt yourself,' he chided, placing his strong hands on her upper arms and drawing her towards him.

The world spun even more, and her sensitive stomach followed suit. 'Nysio... I think I'm going to be sick.'

That was the only warning she managed to give him before she pitched forward and was violently ill all over his designer shoes.

CHAPTER SEVEN

THE ROOM WAS bathed in darkness when Aria awoke. Even with the lack of light, she could tell that this wasn't the same sofa she'd fallen asleep on earlier once she had stopped being sick. Alarm swept through her, followed swiftly by nausea when she tried to shimmy herself across the vast mattress to reach the edge of the massive bed.

The low rumbling sound of someone's breathing made her freeze and alarm had her reaching out to the bedside table for any source of light. A dim reading lamp flickered to life above the bed, casting the room with a soft golden hue. A broad male frame loomed large in the shadows, taking up all of the space upon one of the silk-covered wingback chairs in the corner. It only took her a moment to realise it was Nysio.

He lay reclined with one arm thrown haphazardly above his head, an action that had evidently spread the edges of his robe wide open, revealing a tanned, toned torso. The chair was likely another priceless family heirloom passed down for hundreds of years, a chair she would bet was made for decorative rather than practical use and yet he was using it as a bed while she had apparently stolen his.

Aria shimmied the last few feet across the bed with as much dignity as she could muster until her feet finally dangled over the edge. The drop to the floor was ridiculously high, yet still she managed it and made her way slowly through to the en-suite bathroom. A light flickered on automatically above her head, momentarily blinding her, and she braced her hands on the cold marble cabinets for a moment in case any more of that strange dizziness returned. It didn't.

In fact, she felt mostly fine, other than the noise of her stomach growling after the lack of food she'd consumed at dinner. But still, the thought of eating anything made her want to gag. Aria leaned back against the cool tiled wall and frowned.

It had been a little over four weeks since the night she'd spent with Nysio on the jet. She hadn't had a regular period since going on birth control, so missing her cycle this month hadn't even made her think twice. She pushed away the niggling concern of what else might be causing her symptoms and instead distracted herself with the memories of the previous night when Nysio had held her hair back while she was ill. Not exactly the romantic last night together that she'd hoped for.

'Smooth moves, Dane.' She covered her face, hardly believing she had blown their final night together so spectacularly. And now she was being even more ridiculous by worrying when she had a flight to prepare for. She shook her head, staring at her reflection in the gilded mirror above the vanity. She was still paler that usual, which was saying something considering she had been born with the world's palest complexion. Her eyes were glassy and her hair was…completely beyond salvation. She settled for a quick swish of mouthwash she found in a cabinet and a bracing splash of water on her face before trying to finger-comb her frizz.

Giving up on trying to look presentable, she inhaled a deep breath and opened the bathroom door only to walk face first into Nysio's very warm, very naked chest. The intoxicating scent of him enveloped her with its drugging warmth and she just barely resisted the urge to bury her face in further before sanity intervened.

If this man had still been harbouring any illicit fantasies about her, she was pretty sure she'd done a top-notch job of obliterating any chance she had after last night's embarrassing performance.

He had most definitely seen her at her worst, and when she took a hasty step backwards and reluctantly met his gaze she was met with a strange look on his face that she was pretty sure was pure pity.

'You still look unwell,' he drawled, his voice a husky rasp from sleep.

'You're such a flatterer,' she mumbled, squirming a little under the intensity of his assessing gaze. He seemed to scan her for a moment before moving aside, allowing her space to awkwardly shuffle past him in the doorway. Likely he was keeping his distance, in case whatever she had was contagious. She realised he was still wearing a fancy robe, briefly taking in the dark hair on his chest and realised that he in fact was wearing matching silk lounge pants. It was so quintessentially posh that she would most definitely have smirked and made a joke under normal circumstances. Of course, nothing about their situation was normal, nor had it ever been really.

He stepped back, pulling the front of his robe closed in a way that made Aria wonder if he'd actually heard her thoughts. Or perhaps he thought she was ogling him, which she most definitely was not. Well…it was hard not to look at a body like his, especially when he was flaunting it mere inches from her face.

Realising she had begun to blush again, she folded her arms and tried to ignore how the movement made her chest ache uncomfortably. 'I'm sorry about last night. You didn't have to… mind me.'

'You needed minding.' He reached out and touched her cheek, scanning her face once more. He was looking at her in much the same way she'd seen him analyse his computer screen on the handful of occasions she'd spied him working. As if she were a puzzle he needed to solve and he would get his answers through sheer force of will.

'Well…thank you. I'm fine now. I promise.' She stepped around him, her chest accidentally brushing his forearm. She winced at the pain in the tender peaks. She glanced up to find concern lacing his brow.

'Are you feverish? Can I check?'

She didn't answer, her vacant silence apparently acting as consent for Nysio to step closer to continue playing amateur doctor, his cool hands touching her cheeks and forehead.

'You seem fine, but the doctor will know better.'

'You called a doctor?' She looked up at him, anxiety making her voice sound small and fragile. She only half listened as Nysio wondered aloud if she was experiencing food poisoning…or a viral infection…or maybe even both at once. He continued to talk, listing off the doctor's qualifications as he washed his hands at the small sink, then paused in the doorway of the bathroom to survey her in silence.

Exhausted, she moved to sit on the edge of the bed, only to feel a cool hand upon her elbow, guiding her away from the soft heavenly mattress and into a nearby chair.

He produced a tray, one that she was pretty sure hadn't been there when she'd awoken. Upon it were some paracetamol, some still water and one of those sachets of electrolytes claiming to be berry flavoured but that just tasted like dirty water.

She was silent as he handed her the pills to take while he set about preparing the drink. Then he sat and watched while she swallowed and sipped, his brow furrowed as he appeared deep in thought.

'Is there anything that I can do?' he asked, eventually breaking the silence.

Aria felt her mouth move but no sound escaped. Even as something within her snapped to attention, she shook her head on the pure reflex of not wanting to be a burden. Of not wanting to ask this man for help even though he'd made it quite clear time and time again that he quite liked being of practical assistance. She liked being minded by him too.

He went to get dressed, blessedly leaving her alone for a moment to gather her feelings back into her chest where they were safer and far less likely to make a mess. She closed her eyes, hoping that the doctor would arrive quickly and give her a clean bill of health. Then there would be no more delaying the inevitable. It was past time to get back to normal life.

'Miss Dane…is there a chance that you may be pregnant?'

Aria stared at the pretty blonde doctor who sat perched on the opposite end of the low coffee table in the suite's living area where the dawn light had just begun to filter in through the windows. She blinked, half thinking she'd misheard the question. It was absurd. She was vaguely aware of Nysio's swift intake of breath nearby but couldn't muster the courage to look at him.

'No. *No*... Definitely not. I'm on birth control. I have an implant in my arm.'

'Birth control is not always effective, and you wrote down here that your last cycle was more than six weeks ago. Is it a possibility?'

But as she sat in choked silence, her subconscious continued to analyse the past week and how *different* she'd been feeling. The food aversions, the vague nausea she'd thought was anxiety, the tender breasts, even feeling more exhausted than usual.

'It might be a possibility,' she said hoarsely, the last word coming out as a whisper.

'*Cosa?*' Nysio frowned at her with confusion, then straightened abruptly. 'You think... you might be...'

'No,' she said quickly. 'Well... I shouldn't be.'

'But you might be.' He stared at her, his gaze unflinching, the sharp tilt of his brows utterly unreadable.

She forced herself to meet that gaze, to straighten her shoulders and accept that this was one situation she couldn't currently run from. 'Yeah. I might be.'

Nysio was utterly silent as the doctor listened to her symptoms and gently asked if she'd like to do a quick test to rule it out. She hummed to herself, her feet bouncing of their own accord as she waited and studiously avoided where Nysio sat silently observing.

'But I have a contraceptive implant,' she repeated. 'So this test is just a precaution, isn't it?'

'No form of protection is fully effective against pregnancy,' the doctor said again patiently. Other than never having sex, of course.' She chuckled, clearly finding humour in her own words. Meanwhile Aria was horrified. The other woman smiled softly, her head tilting to one side as she surveyed the small plastic rectangle in her hands.

'Well, it appears we have a very clear result.' She moved closer, placing the test on the surface of the low coffee table between them. 'You are most definitely pregnant.'

Nysio could do nothing but watch as Aria shook her head wildly for a moment before swiftly excusing herself to use the bathroom as if the hounds of hell were at her feet. The unmistake-able sound of retching ensued.

Nysio studied the pregnancy test. It was barely the length of a credit card and only a third of the width with one small plastic screen at the centre. A screen that currently showed two pink lines, side by side.

He paled, composing the rapid thrum of his own heartbeat under his fine silk suit jacket and placing the small test back down onto the table as though it were a bomb, set to erupt any moment. In a way, he supposed it might be, considering the doctor was now studiously avoiding looking at him. He knew that she was a medical professional, but as a man who had lived decades now with people using even the most ridiculous information against him, he felt the swift instinct to protect this delicate new development.

'I'll give you both some time to talk,' the doctor said gently. 'But I'll need to return to remove the birth control. It's a simple proce-dure. I'll talk you both through some more of the details of what to expect then too.'

'Thank you, Doctor. You will receive an ad-ditional payment for your discretion,' he said quickly, grateful when the woman shook his hand and disappeared without any prompting.

Nysio wandered back to the bathroom door, knocking once and noting the stark silence coming from within.

'Just let me know you are still conscious in there.'

A small sound, suspiciously like a muffled sob, came from the other side of the locked door and Nysio felt his chest tighten in response.

'I just…need a moment.' Aria spoke between deep breaths.

Something tightened in his chest at the forced strength in her words. Even now, she was putting on her brave face. The urge to force his way into the bathroom to see that she was okay consumed him, but alongside that was an equally strong urge to run far from this apartment and the momentous life-changing revelations that had taken place.

He took a seat in the living area directly across from the bathroom, feeling the weight of reality pressing in upon him. Before finding out the truth of his birth, he had assumed that once the reserves for their foundations and investments were restored he would settle down and have a family of his own. It was the Bacchetti way, after all, to ensure the bloodline continued no matter what it took. But, of course, he was assuming that this pregnancy was a result of their night on the jet. That might not be the case. That realisation stopped him in his tracks, his gut tightening. Was it even his baby?

He sat frozen for a while longer, until the silence was broken by the sound of the bathroom lock sliding open. Aria emerged, her face wan and flushed and her shoulders sagging with clear exhaustion. Nysio stood, stalking across the open expanse of the living room, and took her gently by the elbow, guiding her to a cushioned armchair with a footstool. Once she was adequately seated, he busied himself with pouring a glass of water and placing it within her reach.

To his surprise she didn't fight him off for fussing, instead she seemed to deflate before his eyes. Her muttering of a limp 'thank you' under her breath was almost enough to have him calling the doctor back.

The question of their situation lay between them in the form of the positive pregnancy test on the coffee table, a gauntlet of sorts, and Nysio tensed as he anticipated her next move. The woman he had come to know over the short time they'd spent together had been a refreshing force of brutal honesty. But this pale-faced version looked weak and cagey, as if she was poised to run from him at any moment. He felt his fingers tighten on the arms of his chair with the effort not to reach out to ensure she stayed put.

Her eyes dropped and she spied the test still lying in the centre of the table behind him. She paused, her lower lip quivering as she averted her gaze, trying to hide her expression from him. The look of vulnerability on it shocked him.

He waited until she finally met his gaze. 'So, you're pregnant.'

'Yes.'

He waited a moment, waited for her to elaborate on that monosyllabic response but no more came. 'Do you have any idea how far along you are?' he asked delicately, watching as she sipped the water slowly.

She closed her eyes for a moment. 'No more than six weeks for sure.'

His own knowledge of reproductive biology was pretty basic but he knew that if she was six weeks along, that put conception right around the time they had first met. He had no idea how many times they had made love that night but he knew it had been…a lot.

One night of abandon.

Was that really all that it had taken for his carefully laid plans to be so thoroughly changed? His recent decision to remain a bachelor was a deliberate one, born of the knowledge that his very existence was a lie and he would never want to inflict that upon another generation.

He kept his voice neutral, seeing the tension in the fine lines around her mouth. He needed to tread carefully, to be tactful. 'That night on the jet you said you had not been with anyone for a long time. Is that still the truth?'

She met his gaze instantly. 'Yes. I…there has only been you for years now.'

He felt her hushed words pierce the breath he hadn't realised he'd been holding. And they stayed there in the air, vibrating through him for a moment with quiet finality. He nodded once. Even though he'd suspected as much, he'd needed to give her the space to confirm it. To acknowledge that there were two of them in this.

A movement jolted him out of his thoughts and he looked up as Aria put her glass down with a heavy *thunk* and dropped her face softly into her hands.

'I know it's not what either of us had planned.' She spoke from between her clenched fingers. 'I know that I have options. But my first thought was that I hope it's okay. I want it to be okay, I want it to be healthy. I know that's probably crazy.'

'It's not crazy. I hope it's okay too,' he said, feeling the truth of his own words.

'It's probably barely the size of a seed. How can something so tiny have such an instant impact on everything?' She looked down at her stomach and he found himself following her gaze. They sat in silence for a moment, the weight of their situation bearing down upon them in equal measure. But then Aria placed her hand unconsciously over her stomach and Nysio felt something raw and primal roar to life within him.

This woman was going to carry his child. They were going to become parents. As progressive as he claimed to be, he felt the urge within him to bundle her close and demand she remain nestled in his bed for the next few months for her own safety. The memory of the night before didn't do much to relax his mood. She had been about to fly back to London this morning, despite his offer for her to stay. She had made her feelings on the matter clear.

Something of the intensity of his thoughts must have shown upon his face because when she looked up at him, she immediately sat up straight and frowned.

'You're not about to demand that we get married or something, are you?' she said, in the same tone that one might ask, 'You're not about to murder me, are you?'

Nysio remained silent, not having considered *demanding* it, as such.

'Is this reverse psychology?' he asked, running his thumb across her knuckles and feeling his eyes drift to the bare skin of her third finger. 'Do you want me to demand marriage, Aria?'

'Of course not!' She stiffened, pulling her hand back and cradling it as though he'd burned her. 'I just thought that's what stereotypical brooding Italian guys usually do in these situations.'

'I've never been in this situation before, have you?'

'No.' She relaxed slightly, but still gave him another sidelong glance for good measure. 'I suppose there's no rush to think about logistics yet. I can still return home today as planned and we can…keep in touch. Make plans on how we can make this work together when the time comes.'

He stood up suddenly, feeling adrenaline fill his veins at her mention of her boarding that damned passenger plane she'd insisted on booking with her own money. 'Do you intend to discuss our child's future via text messages?'

'Don't be cross. It's very early still. We can carry on with our lives as normal, for a while at least.'

'Normal,' Nysio repeated, feeling his pulse quicken as she stood up and walked towards the windows. 'What is normal about the fact that you are carrying *my* child and you're already planning to leave the country before we've even properly discussed it?'

Aria inhaled on a gasp, her fists tightening by her sides as she stared at him for a long moment. 'You sound like a caveman.' She gritted the words, her clenched teeth becoming visible for a moment before she walked away into the bedroom.

He followed her. 'Aria…you cannot claim to want to be together on this while simultaneously walking away from me at every chance.'

'I didn't say I wanted to be together, I said we could *work* together.' She stared at him as though he were the one being completely irrational. 'I have a bank appointment next week about the backing for my lingerie line… I haven't even thought of what effect this is going to have on all of that yet. I just lost a pretty steady job so it's not ideal timing for me to be pregnant... I—I just need some time to think. Can you just give us both that?'

Nysio reached out and placed a hand on her arm. '*Calmate*. Relax. Deep breaths, remember? You need me to count your fingers?'

She let out a weak laugh at the reminder of their first meeting and Nysio decided that questioning her any further in this frame of mind was simply going to make her spiral further.

He folded his arms and watched as she moved past him to gather the things into the case he'd had couriered over from the hotel while they awaited the doctor. With every folded garment she placed in the case, he felt his own resolve tighten. She wanted time, she'd said. Well, he would be the one to give it to her. As much time as she needed to understand why a long-distance co-parenting plan was simply not possible in his world.

Like it or not, Aria Dane had just become a more permanent fixture in his life than he'd ever imagined. A fact that he felt strangely at ease about, for someone who'd been so hellbent on remaining a bachelor for the rest of his days. Having a family might not have been in his plans recently, but now that it was happening, he knew what he wanted.

As he guided her out into his waiting car, he knew that she was not going to be happy with what came next, but if the alternative was letting her leave…he'd risk her anger.

CHAPTER EIGHT

ARIA KNEW THAT she was being too quiet on the drive, that they should be communicating with one another before her flight left, but it had seemed that the reality of their situation was sinking in more and more with every mile, making her hyperaware that there was actually a tiny life growing inside her.

It should be positively illegal for a man to look as cool, polished, and collected as he did in his open-collared black shirt and charcoal trousers combo. His shoes today were a deep tan, embroidered with delicate symbols upon the sides that looked almost like hearts.

His hair was still slightly damp from his shower, and her enhanced sense of smell meant that she could make out every different note of his shampoo. Or maybe she was just imagining that? It was far too early for her to be feeling anything like that, surely.

She closed her eyes, praying that she could hold herself together long enough to get through this goodbye, even as every muscle in her body screamed at her to cancel her flight and stay in Italy for longer. But she couldn't do that. Not when she could tell that Nysio was harbouring some archaic sense of chivalry.

She startled, feeling warmth covering her hands where she had been twiddling her thumbs and picking at her cuticles.

'*Calmate, tesoro.*' Nysio spoke quietly from beside her as he put his hand back on the wheel. 'You will wear your fingers away.'

She looked across at him, suddenly realising that she now carried the heir to an empire that had stretched back for centuries. She had no idea if he had ever planned to have children of his own, if he was as panicked as she was.

'Aria, I can hear your thoughts speeding along. Everything is going to be fine.'

'How could you know that? I've been taking antacids for my nausea all week. I drank a little wine with dinner. I haven't been taking any prenatal vitamins.'

He frowned, nodding once. 'My mother told me she didn't know that she was pregnant with me till she was four months along. She was just eighteen and quite the wild child. I'm sure she did much worse before she found out.'

The admission was effective in stopping her overloaded mind, making her turn her stunned focus on him. 'Were you both okay? Was the pregnancy uneventful?'

'She was an unmarried teenager from an upper-class Sardinian family. Although she married my father pretty quickly, I doubt anything about that time in her life could be considered uneventful.' He let out a harsh laugh that didn't quite meet his eyes. Then he reached out again, taking her hand and waiting until she met his eyes fully. 'She was fine and I was born healthy. And look at me now, a perfect strapping man in his prime.' He let her go and gestured to himself with false bravado, the expression on his face so stern it made her laugh involuntarily. She let out a sigh of relief, nodding once.

Without words, his expression seemed to convey the multitude of emotions passing through her in that moment and she felt the stranglehold of control she'd been clinging to begin to slip.

Aria exhaled a long slow breath and covered her face with her hands, peeking out at him through her fingers. 'I can't even keep a houseplant alive, let alone a baby. Do you know how many ferns I've killed through sheer negligence?'

'Aria, I promise you will not be doing this alone. We will be figuring this out together.'

She looked up at him, feeling a wave of gratitude for the fact that, despite their lack of communication regarding how they would be proceeding, not once had he wavered in his support for her about their unnamed bean. She closed her eyes, thinking she might nap for a bit, but startled when she felt the car jostle off the motorway and onto a narrow mountain road.

'This isn't the way to the airport.'

'We're not going to the airport. We need some time to discuss how things will be, going forward.'

How things will be.

The phrase made her sit up straight in her seat, her throat convulsing slightly as she strained to get words past her fury. 'Turn this car around, *now*.'

He remained stubbornly focused on the road, ignoring her. By the time the car slowed and passed through wrought-iron gates, her muscles were sore from the anxious tension. A large stone wall spanned for miles and she read the words *Palazzo Bacchetti* engraved deep in the stone. Tall cypress trees lined the long avenue in perfect formation, interspersed with tall golden lamps and sculptures. But when they passed through a second set of gates and she was presented with the enormous sprawling palace she stopped breathing for a few seconds.

Nysio Bacchetti lived in a palace. An actual, real-life Renaissance palace.

Her momentary awe didn't last for long though, and when the car came to a stop in the beautiful courtyard, she immediately threw off her belt and stepped out, slamming the door behind her pointedly.

'Aria,' Nysio warned. '*Calmate, per favore.* Stress is not good for you or the baby.'

'Well, then, stop doing things that you know will stress me out!' she snapped. 'I'm not suddenly made of porcelain, simply because I'm pregnant. I will not be ordered around and ferreted away somewhere for safekeeping until I give birth to your heir.'

'You expected me to just allow you to return to England this morning without even discussing our situation properly?'

'You are not in a position to decide what I am *allowed* to do simply because I'm pregnant.'

'Pregnant with *my* child.' His eyes were twin pools of cold obsidian, dark and unwavering. 'I've tried hard to be patient and rational here, so as not to overwhelm you. But I am a very wealthy and powerful man, Aria. There are measures that people in my position need to take to ensure *safety* for their families. To ensure that my vulnerabilities are not exploited or used. Like it or not, you and our baby have just become my biggest vulnerabilities and I have to protect you.'

'So that's it? I don't even have a choice?' She stared at him, feeling her jaw clench.

'You said you needed time. Well, I'm asking for the same. We both want the same thing... space to figure this all out. I'm just asking that we do it here, together, so that I can keep you safe. Both of you.'

She felt caged in, as if she were a bad mother already if she didn't take this time to process and decide upon their child's future. She knew he was right, that there were so many things to decide upon.

Aria stared up at the stone building, the sprawling land surrounding them. Sprawling land that seemed to be surrounded by a very high brick wall as far as the eye could see. She wasn't even sure if they were in the city any more, to be honest, it was so quiet, peaceful and beautiful. A beautiful prison.

Was this really happening?

'I told you I have plans in motion back in London and a meeting with the bank to get to. I can maybe push things out by a week, but that's as much as I'm willing to do.'

'Most people wouldn't see an unexpected stay in this *palazzo* as such a tedious endeavour.' He pushed agitated fingers through his dark curls, his expression shifting. 'All I'm asking for is a little time.'

It felt ridiculous to keep having the same argument over and over again, and so she did something she almost never did. She gave in.

'One week.' She looked up at the façade of the *palazzo*, feeling a shiver course down her spine.

Aria stared around her at gold gilded furniture, luxury marble flooring and priceless portraits lining the walls. For goodness' sake, even the chandelier that hung from the vaulted double-height hall ceiling of the entryway was probably worth more than she had earned in her entire lifetime.

A man arrived at the bottom of the stairs looking rather harangued, but still perfectly coiffed in a spotless three-piece suit. Aria inwardly groaned, recognising him as the same man from the jet on that first night. He recognised her too, his eyes lighting up as he greeted them, and Nysio announced that Aria was to be their guest for the week.

If Gianluca found any of his employer's behaviour to be absurd, he didn't show it. They gave her a short tour of the public areas of the grounds and Aria was glad for the distraction as she cooled off from her heated exchange with Nysio. She fought the urge to swoon at every new room and piece of history she was met with, realising that the father of her unborn child lived in a home that came complete with its own art gallery and staff.

Nysio disappeared for a while, returning when she had just begun settling into one of the many bedrooms in his suite. But not his bedroom, she realised quickly. A fact she should probably be relieved about, now that they were trying to build a co-parenting relationship. Sex would definitely only complicate matters further and that was not the kind of world she wanted to bring a baby into. They needed stability, communication, respect. And she was fast beginning to realise that he was right, they needed time to get to know one another so that they could be a better team.

He stepped into her bedroom, his eyes strangely guarded as he took in her half-unpacked case upon the floor. 'If you have need for more clothing, I can arrange to have a selection sent up from your preferred store.'

'I can drive, you know.'

'I'd prefer if you remain within the grounds. Besides, I have a relationship with most boutiques in Florence and Milan.'

'So…ordering women's clothing is a service that you avail yourself of often?' His brow instantly rose at the snarky question and she felt a little chagrined. 'It's none of my business of course. I know I'm just here as a *guest*, after all.'

'I assumed you wouldn't want me to announce the private details of our situation to my entire staff…but if you prefer, I can call them all back to clarify the exact nature of our relationship.'

She crossed her arms. 'We don't have a relationship, Nysio.'

He gritted his jaw and for a moment she thought he might lean down to close the gap between them. When had they even moved so close to one another? He was so close, she could feel the heat of his breath fanning her cheeks. She felt her pulse quicken, her body instantly betraying her the way it always did when he was near.

She knew that he could feel it too, the sudden shift in the air between them. She reflexively licked her dry lips and saw his eyes darken as he homed in on the movement. But instead of moving closer, he remained stubbornly frozen in place.

He stared down at her, his chest rising and falling with each breath. 'If I wasn't so sure you'd run away at the first chance, I'd have laid claim to you in front of them all. I'm not like that bastard who used you before. I'm not playing games here, Aria…when I said we will be discussing all of our options while you are here, I mean *all* of them. Including the one that involves you wearing my ring on your finger and remaining here as my wife.'

He enunciated the last word with a rough silky promise that sent a shiver coursing down her spine. 'If you think that you can force me into some kind of…old-fashioned marriage of convenience—'

He raised one brow. 'I don't plan to force you into anything. You gave me one week, Aria. I plan to use that time to explore all of our options quite thoroughly.'

CHAPTER NINE

ARIA FOUND HERSELF seated at one end of an opulent ten-foot-long dining table the next morning, being asked how she would like her eggs. Her cup was filled with the richest, most delicious decaf coffee she had ever smelled in her life, and when she tasted it she had to close her eyes for a moment to tackle the onslaught of sheer perfection.

She was alone in the breakfast room, a fact that she was quite grateful for considering how aggravated her esteemed host had seemed the night before when she had declined eating dinner together. She'd needed time alone to think and thought it better to have a simple meal brought to her room so that she could deal with the phone calls she'd needed to make. A quick voicemail to her parents was all she could muster the courage for, just saying that she'd met a friend and decided to explore Italy a bit more.

She'd also bitten the bullet and sent a long rambling series of voice texts to Priya, outlining her new business idea. She knew the plus-size fashion market like the back of her hand, she knew plenty of vendors and production factories. She knew her own designs were good and she had personal experience of having a more voluptuous body and wanting to dress it with the same level of elegance that could be found in high-end boutiques.

She inhaled softly, letting the breath hiss from her chest on a slow pulse. The relaxation technique had been a helpful online suggestion to combat anxiety. After barely two minutes, she stood up, her fists tight with what was decidedly even more restless energy than she'd begun with.

Of all the brooding Italians she had to meet, how on earth had she wound up with the one guy who practically owned a mausoleum? A mausoleum that she was expressly prohibited from leaving. The hallway outside the dining room was thankfully deserted, as was every other long corridor in the sprawling wings of the ridiculously gigantic palace.

She had never been as calm and carefree as when she'd spent time city-hopping and wandering and learning new things about each new place by walking through it and drinking it in with all her senses. Some people described wanderlust as a hobby, or avoiding reality, as her older sisters often laughed. No one back home had probably even batted an eyelid when she'd told them she was staying in Italy with a stranger for an extended break. For a time Priya had been her companion on her travels when they could book time off work, and that had been the happiest, most peaceful she had felt. They had seen so much of the world together, and she had held her friend's hand as she healed from her own past.

Of course, according to her friend's last call to her, now Priya was a newly-wed herself, and busy with starting up her new business venture. In order to access her inheritance, she'd eloped with her former groom's hot blond billionaire brother and now apparently, they were madly in love. She hadn't even mentioned trying to see each other, nor had she apologised for abandoning her in New York…though it sounded as though it had been pretty unavoidable. Aria told herself that was why she hadn't mentioned Nysio or the pregnancy in her voicemail. She could be mysterious too.

Over the past year, maybe even the past few years, she and Priya had drifted apart. Their jobs had become more time-consuming, especially when Aria had been finishing her online degree in every bit of spare time she'd had. She had finally become open about her ADHD diagnosis to her employers and received some modest accommodations to her working schedule. She'd tried a few things to help herself. Medication hadn't suited her at all but taking scheduled walk breaks and using visual timers to complete tasks seemed to help a little. Simply accepting her different neurology had been a huge step in itself, one that had given her the confidence to go back and get her degree and open herself up to her dreams again.

But still, she missed her best friend.

She let her thoughts continue to wander as she walked through the impressive galleries filled with countless historical paintings and sculptures. It was a sin to keep things like this locked away from the public, unable to be appreciated and admired as they'd been created to be. She wondered if Nysio had always kept this obvious slice of history locked up like a fortress, and himself along with it.

She didn't buy his workaholic line; surely a man with his kind of wealth had no need to work full-time hours? Surely he'd feel the urge to spend his money, to own multiple homes,

yachts, islands even? Thoughts of her mysterious host held her attention more effectively
than anything else she'd tried, so she let her
mind turn him over and over like a puzzle. She
almost didn't realise she had reached a completely new part of the house, one that seemed
more modern and quieter than the rest, overlooking the beautiful ornamental gardens to
the rear of the property.

Without a thought, she slid off her shoes and
stepped out onto the cool grass. Rows of vibrant
flowers lined a flagstone pathway leading up
to a large fountain and, beyond, she could see
what looked like a giant maze. She wandered
for a while, happy to let her thoughts run at
full tilt while her body exerted some energy.
It helped sometimes, moving her body to calm
her mind. By the time she walked back towards
the *palazzo*, she felt a little more clarity in her
situation.

Through open patio doors, she spied walls
upon walls of books and in front of them was
Nysio, sitting at an ornate black marble desk.
His hair was dishevelled and falling over his
forehead, but she could just make out a pair
of stylish reading glasses on the bridge of his
nose.

She moved closer, but he didn't hear her footsteps. She debated clearing her throat to announce her arrival, but what would she even say? He had made it quite clear that she was there so that they could take time to discuss the baby, but just barging into his office and demanding they get to it was possibly a little too much for day one? Then again, he had been *so* eager to get her here. Irritation warred with uncertainty as she hovered in the doorway, her bare feet getting cold on the stone.

'My office has an open-door policy, Aria. There is no need to hover.'

His voice startled her; he hadn't once looked up from his work but evidently she hadn't been quite as stealthy as she thought. Slowly, he slid the glasses from his face and placed them down on the desk beside what she could now see was not a live screen of stock markets or accounts but a book with a pregnant woman on the cover. The title read, *What To Expect...* He quickly pushed it out of sight, clearing his throat.

'You look well rested.' His gaze slid down to take in her simple jeans and T-shirt.

She knew he had to be able to see her dark under-eye circles, her hair tied up in a messy bun, and her appearance was infinitely more casual than his sleek white shirt and tailored trousers. 'I'm as well rested as a captive can be, I suppose. Who knew prison cells had four-poster beds?'

The corner of his mouth quirked. 'Your sense of humour has recovered, I see.' He stepped around the desk, lazily propping his lean lengthy frame against the front edge. 'I had thought we might engage in some banal pleasantries before we jumped at one another's throats today, but then I'm reminded that this is infinitely more entertaining.'

'Glad to be of service,' she said dryly, entering the office and feeling his gaze lower to her bare feet. His eyes darkened for a moment on her red-painted toes and she felt a hint of self-consciousness creep in. Being in his fancy home and seeing him in his polished suit, aware of how he very much belonged here...it only seemed to cement the fact that she didn't. She was just the quirky stranger that had entertained him for a while. Even when he'd said he wanted her to stay, he'd wanted to hide her away in his town house; he had never meant to bring her here, into his inner circle.

He'd wanted to discuss all of their options for the baby...but he had already moved them to separate bedrooms without even a conversation and had not once tried to touch her romantically since the night they'd found out she was pregnant. And despite her anger at his heavy-handedness in getting her here…she missed him.

She shook off that vulnerable thought, reminding herself that she had logistics to sort through with this man. Plans to decide upon and details to iron out. This was essentially a negotiation and she needed to be on her guard. 'I decided that I may as well make the most of my time here. Explore the grounds, clear my head.'

'You should have come to me. I'm happy to give you a longer tour.'

'I'm okay exploring alone,' she answered quickly. 'I needed the time to get my thoughts in order. I was already stressed about my business plans, before we found out about…our situation.'

'Is that what we're calling it?' His mouth tipped up at one corner but he remained thoughtful as he watched her. She wandered along one bookshelf, touching the few leather-bound tomes and classics she could recognise by title. She'd never enjoyed reading as a child—it had always felt too slow. Now, she'd found that audiobooks were a little easier to process and she could actually enjoy reading that way. But there was something so romantic to her about a shelf of dusty old books.

'My career problems probably seem a bit trivial when you're managing millions...or billions.'

'Success is a relative concept, in my experience. Even the most outwardly successful people can still be unsatisfied.'

She looked up, seeing a hint of something vulnerable in his gaze. He was the kind of man that gave his full attention to every conversation, a fact that was fast becoming quite disconcerting. He was so observant and so effortlessly polished and articulate. She cleared her throat, taking another few steps into the room, and spotted a large marble chess set that sat propped on a table in the corner.

'Do you play?' he asked.

'My older sisters taught me.' She laughed softly. 'They quickly regretted their decision when I started to beat them every time. My parents had to give away our chessboard to stop the arguments.'

'You have a temper, then?'

'I'm a redhead, most people simply assume that I have a temper.'

'I am not most people.'

Aria blinked, a pithy retort dissolving on the tip of her tongue. She stared around at the rows of thick books that lined the shelves of his study, books that were clearly not just for aesthetic purposes judging by the stack in disarray on the floor beside a tall wing-backed chair near the windows.

'Well, I definitely had a temper as a child.' She sat down at the chessboard, running a hand over the pieces. 'Too little patience and far too much energy. Once I learned that my brain works differently, that part of my life made a lot more sense.'

Nysio frowned, taking a seat on the opposite side. 'Did no one mention ADHD when you were a child?'

'No. My parents are very calm, academically driven people. They didn't understand me and I didn't really want to be understood.' It was hard enough not being able to understand or cope with the challenges without the added pressure of trying to explain her challenges to others. Her three older sisters had been such high achievers growing up, busy with piano concerts and dance recitals and sports tournaments. She frowned, not knowing how she had got onto this topic and why she was oversharing so much. 'Things were very different back then. I don't blame them. Our family has drifted apart a lot, we're not close.'

'It's hard when you don't fit the plan of who your parents want you to be.'

She studied his face, seeing another hint of that restlessness she'd noticed the first time they'd met. 'Is that how yours made you feel?'

'My anxiety attacks have always been a part of me. My father never accepted that I struggled with large events, just told me to be a man. He's old-school that way, he doesn't really believe in talking about feelings or emotions…' A dark look came over his face and he was silent for a long moment.

'It must be hard, with your father's illness and them moving so far away.'

'I had a very privileged life.' He shrugged. 'I was taught to appreciate the position I was born into. I was trained to take over all of this from the moment I could talk so even though I struggled to begin with, I eventually fitted their plan. I am who they needed me to be.'

She remembered his story of the poetry and wondered if he had ever wanted to be something different. If his entire life had always been centred around being this intense Florentine prince…if he had ever been allowed to just be him. It seemed impossibly sad to think of a little boy being *trained* to play a role.

She didn't remember accepting his offer

to play, but suddenly they were both moving pieces on the chessboard. He didn't let her win, and he was clearly an expert player, but she managed to get a few moves in before he hammered her with a quick checkmate.

'One more?' He quirked one dark brow in her direction.

She nodded, feeling the tension in her shoulders ease. And she kept talking, realising that she didn't feel self-conscious at all. Nysio was a great listener, asking questions and letting her interrupt him in her usual way. It was always strangely effortless to talk to him, so much so that she found it hard not to overshare. When he asked again about the reason why she had sworn off relationships so adamantly...she paused for a split second, then decided to tell him the whole story.

She explained about meeting a wealthy older guy named Theo in her first year of uni and the shadowy nature of their relationship. How he'd taken her away on holidays and breaks but never actually been happy to go public about their relationship. How he'd claimed to love her curvy body so much that his occasional sharp comments and criticisms about her size had felt like love. It wasn't until the end that she'd realised how many parts of herself she had bent and broken to try to fit into his expectations both inside the bedroom and out.

She told him about Theo's wild ideas and impulsive traits, how he'd used her and discarded her at will. How she'd always gone back when he apologised…every time. By the time she got to the part where Theo had proposed and booked a wedding in Greece before abandoning her there…she felt that soft wounded part within begin to shake with memory.

She reached down to busy herself with clearing the pieces, accidentally brushing Nysio's hands as he moved to do the same. She had felt the tension in him, but when she looked up, his eyes were stark with anger.

'I'm not a violent man…but if I met this Theo in the street, I'm pretty sure I'd struggle not to dislocate his jaw.'

'A kind gesture, but he got his comeuppance when his trust fund ran out and all of his so-called friends deserted him. Priya was such a great support.' Aria smiled. 'Strange to think my runaway-bride best friend is the only reason you and I met one another. She actually went and married the groom's brother. Can you believe that?'

A strange look crossed Nysio's features, and she realised she hadn't really mentioned Priya or that scandalous wedding since the first night they'd met. She'd got far too swept up in all of the magnificent sex they'd been having, to be fair. Was he uncomfortable at the reminder of his panic attack in the street?

She hadn't spoken to her friend again since the last call they'd had in London, the one where she'd dropped the bomb that she was in fact married. Her husband was a wealthy Greek tycoon named Eros Theodorou, their marriage initially brought on by a ridiculous term in a will and a race to the altar between Eros and Priya's former groom, Xander. A thought occurred to her, one she was amazed she hadn't questioned until now.

'You know that day on the street, I heard Xander send his men in pursuit of his brother.' She waited a moment, noticing the flare of Nysio's nostrils and the slight widening of his eyes. Feeling her gut tighten with foreboding. 'When I saw you first... I wondered if that brother was you. But you said you were only there on business, so I presumed you didn't even know Xander. Was that the truth?'

'No.' Nysio spoke carefully. 'It was not the truth. But I think you've figured that out already. The truth is that Xander and Eros are my half-brothers. We're all Zeus Mytikas's illegitimate sons.'

She gasped. 'You lied to me?' Aria whispered, shaking her head. 'Is that why you offered me a flight home? To ensure that I hadn't uncovered your secret?'

'That wasn't the reason, but it was a consideration that occurred to me only briefly. It soon became pretty clear you didn't know and then…things developed between us. It's not something I've spoken about with anyone, it's not just you.' Nysio felt his chest turn cold, his mind warring with him to walk away from this conversation he didn't want to have. But still, seeing the hurt clearly evident in her eyes made him feel like the worst kind of scumbag.

'Did you know that Priya had married your brother?'

Nysio winced at the word. He'd largely avoided thinking about Eros or Xander at all since leaving New York. Even when he'd received an invitation to attend a meeting with them both to discuss alternative options for that damned will, he'd ignored it. He'd been in the dark about their existence for over three decades; he had no need to play happy families now.

'Yes, I've been made aware that both of my

half-siblings have recently got married in a bid to win an inheritance from Zeus.'

A pained expression passed over Aria's face, marring her soft brow. 'Is that why you want to get married to me? To compete with them for the terms of the will?'

'No,' Nysio growled. 'And I can't believe you even have to ask that.'

'I don't know what to believe.' She let out a low curse under her breath and covered her face with her hands. 'My best friend's husband is your *brother*. Our child's future aunt and uncle. God, I haven't even told Priya that I'm pregnant yet. I… I need to go and lie down for a bit.'

Nysio was silent, allowing her to walk away. Silence was easier than explaining to her the fact that he himself hadn't known about Zeus or his brothers until just before he'd met her on that rainy Manhattan street. He'd been in shock these past weeks, he realised. He'd been like the man in his poem, drunk and grasping around in the dark, determined to make the night sky change back to day. It wasn't going to change the facts, and he'd been foolish to ignore the truth for as long as he had, but everyone processed things in their own way. His way had apparently been furiously clutching to his old reality and completely refusing to acknowledge the fact that so much of his life had been a lie.

Aria had been like a brightly shining star, keeping him from falling further into the darkness. But that was not a burden he could continue to put on her. She was about to have his child, and he had asked her to trust him…and yet he had not shown her that same trust.

The day he had found out the secret behind his birth, he'd lost a part of himself he hadn't even realised he'd treasured. As a young man the burden of being Arturo Bacchetti's only heir had made him restless, but he'd poured his all into reaching his father's incredibly high standards and doing their family proud. Now it felt as if he was just a hair's breadth away from bringing scandal upon the Bacchetti name.

He had barely left this palace in years, and the first time he'd given in to the impulsive temper that always bubbled below the surface of his control it had brought him to Aria. The first woman to tempt him in years. The first woman who had ever come close to making him want to break his own carefully laid-down rules.

Now look where he was.

He had refused to offer her more than a casual affair, then, once he knew she was carrying his child, he had essentially taken her prisoner in his palace so that he could convince her to marry him. He growled under his breath, moving to slam the door closed only to find Gianluca staring back at him from across the threshold.

'Someone is in great spirits, I see.'

Nysio ignored the other man, stalking across the room and sitting down heavily behind his great black desk.

'Your mother called.'

'I don't care,' Nysio growled.

Gianluca grimaced, standing up to place his hands on the desk, forcing Nysio to look up at him. 'Cora knows about the will, Nysio. She knows that you know about Zeus.'

Nysio froze, looking at his father's oldest friend and seeing in his eyes that the other man also knew about Zeus. Of course it would be impossible to hide such a secret from the man who had helped keep the Bacchetti family in check for almost five decades. Gianluca was their most trusted employee, their curator, the man who kept the entire *palazzo* running...he'd seen everything.

'Sit down,' Gianluca urged, a long sigh escaping his lips. 'Let's talk.'

He had assumed that his mother had tricked

his father somehow into thinking Nysio was his baby, that his father had found out the truth and been forced to litigate to protect the family name. He wondered if his father had ever seen him as a disappointment, a cuckoo in his polished nest.

But through Gianluca's eyes, he heard the story of how his parents had been very much in love. But one foolish mistake while they'd been briefly broken up had led Cora to Zeus. Shortly afterwards, she'd reconnected with Arturo and they'd become engaged. She'd been four months pregnant when she found out about the baby, the week before their wedding. She'd told Arturo straight away and handed him back his ring but Arturo had chosen to claim Nysio as his own. And that, according to Gianluca, was where it was always supposed to have ended.

Zeus was a notoriously powerful and cruel man, so the best way to protect Nysio and Cora was to pretend the baby was Arturo's. That had worked, until Zeus had stumbled upon Cora Bacchetti's handsome blue-eyed sixteen-year-old son at an event and secretly had a DNA test performed. The legal proceedings to protect their family had been gruelling and Cora had begged Arturo to tell their son the truth. But he'd refused, not wanting his relationship with his son to be changed. Not wanting Nysio to have to face such a long-buried truth…risking losing their son's trust for ever. They'd been in too deep.

Nysio sat, reluctantly. And he listened to every word, not bothering to hide the tears that gathered in his eyes. By the time an hour had passed and Gianluca finally left him alone with his thoughts, he had an entirely different perspective on the sordid Bacchetti secret that he'd been avoiding thinking about and haunted by for weeks. He'd seen it for what it was, two parents doing what they thought was best to raise their child.

To protect him.

CHAPTER TEN

ARIA AIMED HER knife in a downward arc, feeling a sliver of satisfaction when it sliced the courgette cleanly in two. Offering to help in the kitchen had been a necessary outlet for the hurt she'd stewed over since yesterday's revelations. The only respite from her thoughts had been when the doctor had come back to remove the implant in her arm and explained that Aria would need a scan at the twelve-week stage.

The kitchen was full with staff preparing for a meal-delivery service that she discovered Nysio had delivered daily to a couple of homeless shelters in the city. The scent of bubbling marinara sauce and freshly chopped parsley assailed her nostrils and made her stomach grumble. She had already decided that she would not be dining with Nysio this evening again. He'd sent a note to her room, handwritten with an apology and a request for her to talk to him when she was ready. But she wasn't ready, not when she felt so misled. The memory of how honest she had been, how she'd told him everything about her. Even told him about Theo.

Whether he had meant to lie to her or not, the secrecy was something that cut through the veneer of her confidence more effectively than any knife could.

She shook her head, popping another grape in her mouth and closing her eyes at the utter divinity of flavour that exploded there. She would really need to bring some of these with her when she went home. Food like this just wasn't the same in England. She hadn't had a bad meal since landing here.

She finished chopping the vegetables, chatting away to the chef until the woman went on her break and the other staff went back to their work and once again she was left alone with her thoughts.

An unexpected wave of emotion rose within her and it took everything she had to tamp it back down. Damn Nysio. Damn his suave Italian accent and whatever magical thrall it had held her under. She set her jaw and tried to calm the strange roiling sea within her chest.

The stairs at the rear of the kitchen led down to a basement corridor of sorts, the kind that you might see in a fantasy movie leading down to the dungeons. Did palaces even have dungeons? she wondered, feeling a little trepidation trickle down her spine as her steps echoed on the stone. A large doorway at the end opened up into a cavernous hall. Automatic lighting flickered on at her movement, and for a moment she stood frozen in absolute disbelief at what she saw.

It was some kind of huge underground lair. Well, that was her first thought until the lights along the vaulted stone ceiling began to brighten illuminating rows upon rows of giant barrels.

She walked along the cold stone floor that ran down the centre, looking at the labels upon each vessel, her eyes widening at the years listed upon them. Whatever was inside these things, some of them seemed to be over one hundred years old.

She moved through another archway and into an even smaller stone cellar. The temperature was not cold down here but not truly ambient either. Modern vents were visible in the walls, and small digital thermometers displayed the temperature and time.

A third area revealed itself even further down the impossibly long space. This room was lined with gleaming glass cases rather than wooden barrels. The wine here had already been bottled and labelled, the same brand name that she had seen that first night on the jet and on their dinner table the night before. Viti Di Cora.

Hard footsteps sounded from behind her and she turned just as Nysio's broad-shouldered figure appeared in the archway behind her.

'I saw you wandering down here. I wanted to talk to you...'

Aria looked down at the floor, her feelings still a little sensitive from the revelations the day before. But still, she wanted to talk too. She realised she hadn't given him any time to share the details surrounding his secret. She had no idea how he actually felt about it. So she nodded, accepting his hand on her arm as he guided her further into the belly of the giant mountaintop *palazzo*. 'What is this place?'

'It used to be an armoury, but now it's a wine cellar. One of the most prestigious collections in the country.'

She looked back along the line of vintage caskets of wine from many other labels. 'This is all yours?'

'It is.'

'I will admit, I have absolutely no idea why anyone needs this much wine.' She made an attempt at laughter. 'But far be it from me to judge.'

Nysio opened up one of the sliding glass doors by pressing a series of buttons that revealed a small pad on which he pressed his thumb. Aria felt her brows rise a little higher. 'Who needs a bionic lock for his drinks cabinet?'

'To call these caskets mere drinks would be akin to calling the *Mona Lisa* a doodle.'

'Well, well. I've always wondered what fancy old wine tasted like.'

He looked adorably aghast. 'These are not for consumption.'

'Seriously?' She frowned. 'That's like buying cupcakes only to display them for a hundred years on your mantelpiece. That's torturous. Surely a good wine exists in order to be consumed?'

'I don't disagree. However, this particular collection is more of a museum and about preservation than simply owning something expensive in order to possess it.'

'Ah.' She nodded. 'Books, chess sets, wine… you do like collecting things, don't you?'

'Wine has long been a passion of mine.'

'Really, I'd never have guessed, what with the seventy million barrels of it lining the bowels of your palace.' She laughed, stopping when she saw he hadn't joined her. Was she imagining it or was he just a little sheepish at his own passionate admission?

'Clearly you have a favourite brand.' She gestured to the opposite wall.

'Viti Di Cora is certainly my favourite, but mostly for vanity reasons.' He pulled a bottle from the top shelf. 'I'm probably biased, considering it's mine.'

'When you say yours, you mean…'

'I make it. Well, it's a collaborative effort, of course. But the grapes are grown on our vineyard in Sardinia where my parents reside. The land there has belonged to my mother's family for more than a hundred years. The grapes are a very specific variety, one that produces quite a unique…' He paused. 'Ah… I apologise. I'm probably oversharing.'

'No, I'm fascinated, to be honest. I know absolutely nothing about wine other than which colour to order for fish or meat. Even then, I always forget.'

'I know far too much about it, as evidenced by our present surroundings.' He looked uncertain for a moment, running a hand through his hair, his eyes suddenly very focused on the stone-patterned ceiling above them.

'Nysio, is something wrong?' she asked.

'Yes.' He exhaled. 'Well, no. I simply came down here to speak to you…about yesterday. To apologise. I know how closed I am about the topic of my birth…the truth is, I'm still processing it. I only found out that Zeus Mytikas was my biological father after his death, when I received a copy of his will.'

He needed to walk as he spoke, a feeling she knew all too well and so she took his hand and allowed him to lead the way back through the cellar and out onto the terrace at the rear of the kitchen. The evening light was dim, so it was hard to make out his expression as he told her the full story from start to finish. How he'd been raised to carry on his father's name, how he'd always suspected he was a bit different but had never questioned it. He'd known his parents had married because of an accidental pregnancy, but he hadn't known that his mother had been carrying another man's child.

'My mother knows that I received the will… she will likely descend upon the *palazzo* if I don't go to Sardinia to address the matter. But… I'd already been avoiding visiting too often, as seeing my father grow more and more ill with every visit is devastating. Now, how am

I supposed to interact with him…knowing he was never truly my father?'

'Sounds to me like he was your father in every way that matters,' she offered helpfully. 'I'm pretty sure that I'm both of my parents' biological child and I've never felt like I belonged amongst my siblings. It seems like maybe you were smothered with belonging…a little bit. But it was done with love.'

He nodded, his jaw tight as he stared out at the setting sun.

'You can't hide from your parents for ever,' she said softly.

'I don't want to waste any of the time you have left here.'

'I could come with you. Your parents will need to know the news of the baby eventually. It's their grandchild, after all. Why not now, while I'm here?' She shrugged. 'It could help me to understand this family better…or worse. I'm not sure. I just know that I don't want to let you go through something so difficult alone.'

'I'd like for you to see the vineyard,' he mused, still lost in his thoughts. 'And we still have a lot to discuss.'

When he walked her back to her room, it was to lay a single kiss upon her cheek and wish her a goodnight before disappearing into his own room. She stood frozen in the hallway, feeling foolish that she had expected him to come inside. That she had hoped he would. The thought of spending another night alone with him nearby was torturous to her overheated libido.

Was he trying a new tactic to get her to agree to what he wanted? Using their chemistry as a bargaining chip? Of course, she hadn't expected him to do something so ridiculous as fall in love. Men like him were probably used to using and discarding women at will. Having one of those women fall pregnant was probably his worst nightmare. She should be grateful for his honesty. But as she walked back into her room alone, she felt the urge to give in to his demands pulling at her stronger than ever. Would it truly be so terrible to become his wife?

The Bacchetti family's Sardinian *castello* was an expansive property built into the edge of a cliff overlooking the sea surrounded by acres upon acres of farmland and vineyards. Cora and Arturo Bacchetti greeted them at the bottom of the steps, hand in hand. The beautiful brunette was much younger than her husband but seemed very much in love as she ensured he was strong enough to walk the few steps across the courtyard to greet them.

Aria stood awkwardly to one side, unable to understand the flurry of Italian that flowed as Nysio leaned in to offer his mother a stiff hug. The tension was palpable and Cora made a visible attempt at holding in her emotional reaction to her son's arrival but the small woman eventually crumbled when Nysio hesitated, then carefully leaned in to place the customary kisses upon his elderly father's cheeks.

Nysio seemed frozen for a moment, he and Arturo standing side by side, as loud sobs filled the courtyard. Aria cleared her throat, urging him with her eyes to do something, to offer his mother comfort. He took the hint, swooping in to embrace the tiny woman with his broad frame. Hushed words in Italian followed between the three and Aria realised that there was to be no preamble, no polite British cup of tea or beating around the bush. These Italians were just diving into their family trauma right here in the driveway. After a long while, the crying stopped and Aria felt the spotlight turn back to her.

The stranger in their midst.

But instead of introducing her politely, Nysio murmured something in Italian, gesturing towards her and making an unmistakeable motion towards her stomach.

'*Diventi* Papa?' Cora cried, moving to swing her arms around Aria's shoulders before switching into broken English. 'I am so happy I cry again. Welcome to the family, *bellissima.*'

Aria barely had a moment to process *that* comment as they were bustled inside and immediately presented with a table full of food and cold drinks, including a strong red wine.

'Little bit is good for the baby,' Nysio's father assured her, his hands shaking slightly as he filled the glass to the brim. They weren't at all what she expected, considering the *palazzo* she'd just come from. But it seemed the quiet island life suited them. Arturo's nurse arrived a short while later and she heard Nysio ask if the staff had sent their things to his master suite.

'Wait just a minute.' She hurried after him. 'I understand that this big family reunion is all about you and I'm totally here to support you in that. But since when are we sharing a room again?'

Nysio had the decency to look chagrined. 'My father presumed that we're engaged and had the master suite made up for us.'

Aria paused and stared up at him, feeling her chest flutter with discomfort. His father assumed she was his fiancée. And he hadn't corrected it? *'Welcome to the family,'* his mother had said to her. *Oh, my God.* Once they got safely behind a closed door and away from prying ears she was going to kill this man.

He conveniently climbed the sprawling stone staircase two at a time, leaving her to huff and puff her way up in his wake as she fumed. Aria looked out of a narrow medieval-style window on the stairway and saw colourful market stalls being erected along the winding streets in the distance.

But that bubble of excitement was quickly popped when Nysio took one look at her lightly fanning herself in the pleasant breeze and growled. Literally growled.

'Merda. You're too hot.'

'Thank you, I try.' She stepped around his glowering form and moved to inspect a giant painting on the wall. Her view was torn away as Nysio turned her to face him, placing his hand on her forehead.

'None of your jokes. I read in one of the books that getting overheated can be bad for you and the baby.'

'I'm not in danger of getting overheated. It's late autumn.' Aria pushed his hand away gently, feeling her chest flutter a little at his concern. 'So you're…reading pregnancy books?'

'Of course,' he said simply. 'I now know what to expect now that we are expecting. At least, up as far as the second trimester. I haven't quite braved the birthing chapter yet.'

Aria realised she had been completely avoiding looking into the details of what lay ahead of her. Maybe she should download some of those books on audio…was she already being a bad parent by not doing her homework? She brooded, her mood taking even more of a downturn as she trundled along in his wake. If he noticed, he said nothing but the moment they had entered his wing he set about opening doors and producing a glass of cool lemonade from somewhere.

His eyes, however, remained steadily focused upon her. But as he watched her, she felt his gaze shift momentarily from practical and assessing to something else that she found infinitely harder to compose herself before. She was relieved when he disappeared to talk to his head of staff so she took her time testing out the gigantic four-poster bed in the centre of the room. Her feet ached and her body felt heavy, the beginnings of a headache forming in her temples.

She looked down, realising she had once again been cradling her gently curved but not yet especially different abdomen. She was barely even seven weeks pregnant, after all, she wouldn't be seeing any rounded bumps for months yet. But this time she didn't correct herself and allowed her hand to rest there, closing her eyes as she imagined what lay ahead. She opened her eyes to find Nysio in the doorway, his eyes trained on the spot where her hand rested.

She straightened instantly, embarrassed at being caught in her private moment. But his gaze trailed over her with a look that seemed perilously close to tender and she felt a lump form in her throat. Suddenly, the thought of growing huge with his child while he possibly paraded other women around his huge palace just seemed a little cruel. Maybe she should tell him that. She should *definitely* tell him that.

Boundaries were important in this situation, after all. For the baby, when they came to visit, she corrected herself. She looked up and for a split second she saw nothing but raw sensual hunger, filled with echoes of moments she'd tried to forget. They had only spent a few stolen nights together and yet she felt this undercurrent of need crackling to the surface with each moment they spent alone.

Something hot and needy thrummed to life within her but she tamped it back down with a brisk clearing of her throat. She could have sworn that Nysio smiled for a split second, a small sigh escaping his firm lips.

'So…your parents think that we're engaged.' She pinned him with her most serious gaze, refusing to be distracted by her own body's reaction to him.

'My father has enough to deal with without being upset by our untraditional situation. My mother has already been told that you rejected my proposal.'

'You didn't propose, Nysio. You…demanded. There is a difference.'

He shook his head, a low laugh escaping his lips. 'If you thought that was a demand…you have a lot to learn about me.'

'You're only proving my point. We know so little about one another.' She moved towards the windows, staring out at the sea crashing into waves in the distance below. 'Coming here won't change anything, not when we are both so different.'

She felt him move behind her, felt his presence inches from her back, begging her to sink into his strength and rest.

'You see our differences as an obstacle, whereas I see them as the very fire that drew us together. We could have a wonderful marriage, *dolcezza*.'

'Marriage is about more than sex, Nysio.'

'You seem to have a great many opinions on the institution. Is your resistance truly about us, Aria, or is it about that spoilt man-child who broke your heart?'

'I don't want to talk about him again,' she said swiftly, turning from him to stare out at the waves as they crashed into the cliffs directly below her window. 'I'm here to support you, to spend time with you until my week here is up.'

'You think it's fair that I'm being held accountable for the wrongs of someone else and now our child—'

'Our child doesn't need their parents to be married. *You* need it. As you made evidently clear today when you didn't challenge the assumption that I was your fiancée just to avoid an uncomfortable conversation.'

'What matters to me is that my child is born into a home with both of their parents. Yes, it's also about tradition and image, but marriage is the most clear-cut way to obtain that.'

When she didn't answer him, she felt him sigh heavily, his breath tickling the back of her neck. How could she feel so furious at someone, and still want them this much? It was absurd and unhealthy. She closed her eyes, deciding distance was the only way she would survive this man.

She kept her voice calm, turning to face him fully. 'Don't you have vineyard duties to attend to?'

'I was hoping to take you out with me, to show you the groves.'

'I'm tired, Nysio.' She sighed. 'I'll see you at dinner.'

He nodded once, moving towards the door. He paused under the archway for a long moment, one hand braced on the frame so tightly his knuckles glowed white. 'I'm sorry I didn't tell my father the truth about us. I already regretted forcing your hand to get you to stay in Italy with me...but once I had you here, Aria... I didn't want to let you go. If you believe nothing else, believe that.'

Then he was gone.

CHAPTER ELEVEN

ARIA WAS FALLING APART.

It was their second day in Sardinia and, true to his word, Nysio had given her space. He'd had the sofa bed made up in their adjoining living room and slept there. She'd listened to the sounds of him tossing and turning in discomfort all night, but he hadn't complained once. When she'd awoken this morning, he was already up and walking the grounds slowly, his elderly father by his side deep in conversation. She couldn't help getting emotional at the sight.

She'd also taken the opportunity to get some work done, checking her emails and voicemail and finding that Priya had been trying to contact her for days. She and Eros were taking a trip to Europe and she wanted to meet up. She could tell by her friend's tone that she was checking up on her. Her finger hovered over the button to return the call, her shoulders sagging with the effort of having to speak. Of having to explain the details of why she didn't really want to meet up. It was too much right now, everything felt like too much.

Feeling the onset of her anxiety reaching a peak, she threw on her sneakers and set about wandering through the groves of olive trees, feeling strangely disconnected from such beautiful surroundings. She didn't know how long she'd wandered alone, until she turned and found herself faced with another wall of fresh green olives rather than the exit she'd expected. At her height, the house wasn't visible over the branches, and neither was the sound of the sea particularly loud enough to guide her.

She was lost.

Panic threatened to overwhelm her completely until the sound of footsteps crunched from behind her. She turned to find Nysio striding towards her, his hair windswept and so long it reached the collar of his sleek riding jacket. Breath sagged from her lungs as she ran to him, burying her face into his chest. He and his mother had gone out horse-riding on the beach after lunch, an activity Cora had informed her quietly that they hadn't done in years.

Remembering the look in the older woman's eyes as she'd quietly thanked her for bringing her son back to life…it had tightened something painfully in Aria's chest that had refused to loosen since. As she looked up at Nysio's handsome face, another fresh wave of tears filled her eyes.

His strong arms enveloped her so tightly, soothing away the raw edges of her panic from moments before.

'Did you get lost? This place is like a maze,' he murmured, holding her even tighter.

'I did. But I'm not crying over that… I don't think. I can't stop crying today. Stupid hormones,' she sobbed, feeling the moisture flow from her eyes, dampening the front of his soft jacket.

This was mortifying, being so wildly out of control of her own body. She was used to feeling her emotions more than others seemed to feel them, but since she'd been pregnant everything seemed so much more intense. But right there, in the midst of it all, was Nysio, his eyes filled with that steady, ironclad warmth.

'I'm right here, *dolcezza*. Just let go,' he said softly, running one hand along the length of her hair from crown to shoulder. It wasn't a sexual touch, it was comforting. It was understanding. He did understand how she felt, she realised. He always had. Her breath exited her lungs in a gust and she let her body sag against him, her softness welcomed against the safety of his hard, broad chest.

She didn't think, she just did what he said, she let go. She let go of all the pent-up emotion inside her, feeling it cascade outwards on a wave. Her chest heaved with it, with the raw break of everything she'd held inside. The obsessive pull towards this infuriating man and the confusing world of his that she'd walked into. The panic for the tiny life growing steadily within her. An innocent being that she had no idea if she would be enough for.

When she finally became aware of her surroundings again, it was to find that Nysio had guided her under the cover of a gazebo in the centre of the olive grove, and produced a handkerchief from his coat pocket. It was so old-fashioned for him to carry such an item it made her smile softly through the sobs that still racked her chest.

She sat still as he wiped under her eyes gently, overcome with tenderness at the realisation that he was caring for her in such a simple and beautiful way. The handkerchief came away black with mascara and she knew she must look like a sight but she didn't care. She was looking at him, truly *seeing* him, and she couldn't look away.

'This pregnancy has just opened up every wound I thought I'd healed. The worry…it hasn't stopped. I never worry. I'm the queen of laid-back.'

'You expect to still hold that title after that tidal wave of anxiety?'

She laughed, feeling something lift within her, leaving a lightness that felt dangerously close to hope. He had a way about him that made her want to relax and trust someone else for the first time in her adult life. She thought of his proposal again, only this time she didn't feel a cold sweat coming on. Was she actually tempted to consider it?

Could they try to make things work together or was it just her hormones talking? In her mind's eye she imagined a life she'd only dared to dream of, a family of her own. A home filled with laughter and joy. But she needed to know that he wanted to marry her for her and not just for the baby or to keep his traditional parents happy. While she knew that she would be fine if she chose to go down the single-parent route…choosing Nysio was infinitely more of a risk to her heart. Was she being selfish by holding back from the possibility of being hurt?

Could she truly trust her own judgement again?

'I cried a little when I saw you walking with your father this morning, how you care for him. Your love for your family…it's beautiful.'

'Do you include yourself in that yet?' he asked.

'I'm not foolish enough to include myself in your family, Nysio.' She swallowed over the sudden lump in her throat, laying a hand over her lower stomach. 'But I trust you to care for your child. To love them.'

'You weren't carrying our child on the first night we met.'

'That was different. You were still…honourable.'

'Not that honourable, considering I couldn't keep my hands off you.'

'Well…yes. But we both felt that madness that night.'

'It's not madness. And it wasn't just that night, Aria. I've wanted you from the moment I saw you on that rain-soaked street and I have not stopped wanting you since. Not once.'

'Nysio.' She shook her head, knowing she felt the exact same way but still telling herself to wait, to be cautious. She was afraid to take that risk again, especially as this time there was more than her heart at stake. There were her child's feelings to consider too. 'I didn't think you wanted me any more.'

'I know I forced you to walk away from your plans in London so that I had more time to ensure that I could keep our child safe. But I haven't stopped fantasising about having you again, not once. I've been half mad with lust, having you so close. You've haunted my dreams…my days…every moment I'm not touching you is torture.'

She remembered his words in the car, when she'd thought he was driving her to the airport. She'd thought him arrogant and high-handed, expecting her to be grateful that he was protecting her when she'd thought he was acting purely in his own best interests. She'd thought she had misread all of the signs that there had been something good between them, something real.

'Put me out of my misery, *bellezza*. Kiss me.'

Nothing could stop her from doing that in that moment. Aria leaned forward, her lips touching his with the softest reverence as she felt his arms slide around her waist and pull her close.

Of all the kisses they had shared in the short time they had known one another, this one was quite possibly her favourite. Not because it was becoming increasingly steamy and frantic in a public place, or because things had been so fraught between them for the past week as they navigated their new situation. But as Nysio's tongue slid over hers, his teeth nipping her bottom lip and his hands caging in either side of her neck, she felt all the feelings that she had tried to deny build up within her to a fever pitch. Not just the raw sensuality that he brought out in her, but the emotion too. It choked her throat, bringing moisture to her eyes and stealing the breath from her chest.

But before she could examine it too closely, he pulled a thick blanket from a chair onto the floor of the gazebo and laid her down on it, and began to draw the skirt of her dress upwards.

'We can't do this here,' she chastised with a little moan as he began to slide her underwear to the side, his intent clear as he licked his lips and stared down at where she was swollen and ready for him.

'They know not to disturb us,' he growled. But instead of stopping what he had just begun, he simply switched up the method, sliding a finger between her sex and swirling in gentle circles that made her sigh in delight.

'Just let me give you this,' he murmured

against her lips, his hands still working their magic between her thighs. 'Just let me remind you why we're so good together. To think that you could ever believe me to have lost interest in you…is madness. If you knew how much you consume my thoughts on a daily basis you'd never accuse me of such a thing.'

'Is this a punishment?' She gasped as the first wave began to build deep within her and he showed no sign of stopping.

'Perhaps,' he murmured, 'or maybe it's just a reminder. One that I am only too happy to give you every single time that you doubt my attraction to you.'

His words struck a chord within her, alarm bells sounding. But they were swiftly drowned out as her orgasm began to build and melted all coherent thought from her mind.

Then he paused and she nearly screamed with frustration.

Nysio was delicate with her, but firm as he pinned her hands and pulled her down gently onto their blanket once more. She was flushed and gorgeous, her newly swollen breasts and darkened nipples peeking out from the top of her bra.

'I want nothing between us.' He leaned

down, licking the barely visible little bud once before taking hold of the front clasp. 'I want to see you, *cara*. All of you.'

He waited for her to tense up, to mention any one of the numerous reasons why he probably shouldn't be making love to her at this very moment, in this place. But she simply smiled, a shy smile filled with a raw vulnerability that took his breath away. Then she reached up and replaced his hands with her own, unclipping the clasp and baring herself to him, then shimmying the rest of her dress down and away.

Nysio swore his erection suddenly gained a heartbeat all of its own as he gazed down at the visual feast laid out before him, making him heat up to self-combustion point with lust. Perhaps she couldn't see the changes that pregnancy had brought to her body yet, but he could.

Her breasts had already been full, but now they barely fitted in his hands. Their tips were the colour of his favourite sweet pink grapes, begging to be tasted. In fact…he reached over and put action to the thought. He swore they tasted better than vintage wine.

He realised he must have spoken his thought aloud when she gasped and said, 'You…really are obsessed with wine.' She made an attempt at laughter, but her breath caught, her hips undulating as his tongue darted out to flick one hardened peak, her breath hissing through her teeth.

'Obsession is not enough to describe what I feel,' he growled, his eyes pinning hers as he bent to kiss each sweet pink bud again. 'I... adore it. I worship it. I fear that I'll never get enough.'

Her eyes held his and he knew by the slight flicker of uncertainty there that she understood. A part of him whispered that he should slow down, that he should continue to show her that she could trust him. But another, much darker part of him just wanted to know that she felt the same.

She still had her eyes half closed, her hips undulating with barely restrained need. She was so responsive, so effortlessly sensual, he could read her without a word spoken. It had been this way that first night, he remembered. He kissed her, fighting the urge within him to push her once again, to demand that she agree to his terms. That she stay in Italy by his side as his wife, in his *palazzo*, in his bed... He fought against the tightness in his chest, the need to possess her completely.

He took his time, whispering his adoration

against the skin of her thighs as he made his way to the silk covering of underwear she wore. The intricately embroidered red silk was dark with her moisture and he couldn't resist laying the first of his kisses against the fabric.

'Wait,' she whispered, her eyes wild with pleasure as she reached down to unbutton his jeans. 'It's always about me. Let me give you pleasure for once.'

He lay back on his side, his fingers still idly stroking her even as she withdrew his hard length and held him in her hands. She stared at him, her tongue darting out to lick her lips for a split second before she shyly leaned forward to press a kiss against him.

From their position lying side by side, top to tail…it seemed only natural for him to mirror her movements, pressing an answering kiss against her centre. She smiled, getting braver by the minute, and took him deeper, almost making him lose control completely.

'*Amore mio*, if we continue this I won't last.' He groaned. 'And I want to be able to feel you around me.'

'I want that too, but right now I want you to lose control like this…from me.'

Nysio needed no further convincing and spread her wide for deeper access. They continued their erotic game of mirrors until he felt her body tighten and tasted her shuddering climax, his own body thrusting wildly as he found his release at the same moment between her lips. Her answering sigh of pleasure vibrated through him, connecting him to her. Joining them together just as they were meant to be and he knew he would never let her go.

CHAPTER TWELVE

EACH DAY THEY spent in Sardinia seemed to challenge so many of Aria's reasons behind not wanting to accept Nysio's proposal. He showed her his sensitive side, showed her his love for his family and his passion for the vineyards and produce that came from Viti Di Cora. She met his extended family on his mother's side, who all lived close by in the small town and worked in the vineyard. She watched while Nysio rolled up his sleeves and got his hands dirty during the harvest. It was like living in a different world and he seemed a completely different man now that he was away from all the duty and pressure from the *palazzo*. He'd even reached out and contacted his half-brothers, at her urging, and a tentative connection was being formed.

When he asked her to stay a little longer...to try to move her bank appointment out another week or two...she accepted without question.

Suddenly the thought of leaving him and returning to London felt completely wrong. So instead, they returned to Florence, as Nysio had commitments he had to honour.

Aria rationalised that Italy was a much better place for her to be while planning out the manufacturing process for her lingerie line. It was the heart of the fashion world, after all! But when she suggested that maybe she could take a trip out to some factories to learn more, Nysio seemed less than enthused. He was a busy man, she understood that. She'd quickly seen just how busy he was between the curation of the Bacchetti collections of art and jewellery that required his signature. Then there was the property arm of their company, not to mention the numerous charities, scholarships and community projects. He worked long hours too, with the stock markets opening and closing at odd times. But still, once he eventually slid into bed beside her, their lovemaking was as passionate and exciting as ever. She could hardly remember why she'd had hang-ups about things like oral pleasure because, well…it turned out that Nysio was an expert in that arena. Her happiness would be complete if he'd even hinted he felt more for her than desire.

Aria stepped in front of the mirror in the *palazzo*'s master suite and took a final look at her reflection. The long red gown fitted her curves to perfection, the material like a second skin over her breasts and waist before flowing out from her hips to the floor. For all of her insistence that agreeing to stay here for the past week was not her agreeing to become the lady of the palace…she felt surprisingly regal.

The Bacchetti annual charity event was in full swing as she descended the stairs alone. Nysio had said he had a surprise for her to attend to. Nerves jittered in her stomach as she wondered what that could be. But before her foot had left the last step she found out as a familiar silhouette with long black hair came barrelling across the hallway through the crowd.

'Priya?' she squeaked, the only sound she managed to get out before she was embraced in a tight hug and cloud of perfume. They stood like that for far too long, their frantic voices only half intelligible as they apologised to one another for the past couple of months of silence. When they finally pulled away there were tears in both of their eyes.

'Damn it, I'm going to ruin my make-up.' Aria took a deep breath. 'I wish this party wasn't going on now, we've got so much to catch up on.'

'We'll talk properly later. Xander is here too, with his new wife Pandora. It seems we both wound up madly in love with gorgeous men, so I guess things worked out.' Priya raised one brow. 'So…you're dating a guy who lives in an actual palace. Let's at least mention that?'

Nothing got past this woman, she saw everything and far too much. As was evidenced by the way her eyes instantly narrowed when Aria smiled and refused a glass of champagne from a passing waiter. The headache that had been plaguing her all week had held off a bit today so she felt mostly fine, once she kept eating and didn't try to stand up too quickly. But when another waiter appeared with a tray of fresh seafood hors d'oeuvres, she felt her entire body threaten to revolt.

'Are you sure you're not ill?' Priya asked quietly, her brow furrowing.

'I'm fine.' Aria scowled, but inside her heart warmed at the obvious concern in her best friend's face. She inhaled a calming breath; now was not the time to tell Priya about the baby. She would need more time and privacy for that conversation. 'Look at us, standing at the sidelines of a party while you play mother hen…it almost feels like we're back in college.'

Priya laughed and Aria felt her body relax at the sound. The whole runaway-bride incident had put pressure on their usually easy relationship. But her friend was happy, as was evidenced by the soppy grin that slowly transformed her face at the sight of the tall blond man crossing the room towards them.

'Your husband is looking quite god-like,' Aria murmured dutifully. 'Now, allow me to go mingle before you two start making besotted eyes at one another again.'

'It better be more than eyes, with all the effort I put into this outfit.' Priya winked, pasting on a bright smile just as her husband reached her side and drew her into his arms for a kiss that bordered on scandalous.

When had her friend become so sultry? Aria forced herself to look away from the easy display of wedded bliss, feeling something shamefully akin to jealousy burn in her gut. Or was it just another bout of nausea? She honestly didn't know which might feel worse in her present state of exhaustion.

She wandered through the crowd of well-dressed guests, taking in designer shoes and tailored trouser cuffs as she followed the mosaic path towards the bar for some water. She didn't know what made her pause and redirect her gaze towards the opposite end of the room.

Nysio stood alone under an open archway at the entrance, his eyes sharply assessing the crowd around him until he spotted her. He was by her side in an instant, taking her by the hand and drawing her away from the mass of people that stood around, admiring the Bacchetti art collection and impressing one another with their knowledge.

'Where are we going?' She laughed as he continued to be mysterious, guiding her along the flagstone path, past the fountain until they were walking deep into the maze she had admired so many times from their bedroom window. The late November breeze was cool on her skin but not unpleasant as they pressed deeper, only coming to a stop when they reached the centre where a small gazebo lay surrounded by illuminated water features and statues.

'Every good maze needs a monster at the centre,' she mused, idly running her hand over one polished marble beast.

'This palace has more than enough of those,' Nysio said.

Something in his voice made her pause.

'You're not a monster, Nysio,' she said, putting as much steel in her tone as she could manage.

'You're sure about that?' His voice echoed around her, that same haunted darkness in his eyes.

'You're not a monster,' she repeated, needing to say this to him, needing him to know how wrong he was to see himself as the product of a tyrant's seed and his father's desire to keep a scandal quiet. 'The monsters are the ones who seek to hurt people. Being overprotective and making decisions out of fear doesn't make you a bad person. But refusing to change your behaviour when you learn that it's hurting someone is.' She raised one brow, leaning down to press a gentle kiss against his forehead.

She moved to walk away but he grabbed her hand at the last minute, holding tight and pulling her into the circle of his arms. 'I brought you here to ask you something.'

The words were murmured against her hair, and for a long moment there was nothing but silence between them, nothing but the strength of their embrace and the beating of her heart.

'I've waited for the right moment to give you this, waited to be sure that you felt happy here. That you could see our future as clearly as I can. These past few weeks have shown us both just how right we can be together when we're working as a team…' He pulled a ring out from his pocket, a beautiful gold band with a giant ruby at the centre. Aria felt her chest hammer, the headache intensifying in her temples as she panicked.

'Aria…will you marry me?'

Nysio knew he had misjudged the situation even before Aria shook her head sadly. He tried to hold in his anger, his confusion, tried to wait for her to explain. Because he fully expected an explanation.

'Nysio… I'm sorry but I can't marry you.'

'Can't or won't?' he growled. 'You would just so easily refuse to be my wife, when you could have access to everything that you need?'

'Everything?' she asked, tilting her head. 'So if I decide I want us to move back to London to open up my own fashion label there like I'd planned?'

His eyes narrowed. 'You're being deliberately obtuse.'

'If I wanted to take our child out for a walk in the park without any security guards? If I wanted to show them how to ride a train, or just take a spontaneous trip to the beach?'

'I admit that our security protocol is heavy, but it is necessary as you know in order to ensure—'

'Safety,' Aria finished for him. 'Yes, I know. You have talked of nothing else from the moment we first met. I can't resign myself to living a life of imprisonment.'

'You still believe me to be keeping you prisoner?' He raised his voice, gesturing at the opulent grounds around them. 'If this is a prison, then I'm right here with you. You believe me to be some poor soul trapped in a life of luxury?'

'Do you feel free?' she asked quietly. 'You seemed free for a moment back there, in Sardinia on your vineyard... For a moment, I thought that perhaps things might actually work out for us. But then we came back here, to this place, to this world and this way of life that you refuse to see is not making you happy. I know you made a promise to your father, and I understand that loyalty is deeply important to you. But it's just not who I am. And it's not the kind of life that I want for our child, being raised to carry on the Bacchetti name without a care for who they are inside. When you jumped straight to wanting marriage for the baby's sake it was easy for me to say no. Because I was terrified of how you made me feel. I was terrified of how much you made me hope and want for more. I do want more... But I cannot be your wife. Not when I know that the only reason you're asking me is to ensure that I stay here, at the *palazzo*, with our child. I'm sorry. You deserved that choice as a boy and our child deserves that now.'

'You will not take my child from me, Aria.'

'Never. I would never do that to you. I promise you that I won't run away, I won't hide from you. Because I know that, despite the bounds of loyalty that you have to the Bacchetti history, you're going to be a good father and you want the best for your child. So, I'm prepared to compromise and find a way to raise this baby with love even if we're not together.'

'So that's it? We're done? I don't have any further say in it?'

She lowered her eyes. 'I… I'm sorry.'

As Aria walked out of the maze and back towards the *palazzo*, she thought she heard a loud curse erupt from the depths of the maze behind her, but then there was nothing but the echo of her own footsteps on the stone steps that sounded like just how she felt inside.

An overwhelming sense of anxiety rose within her, and she found herself unable to speak as she entered the front door of the *palazzo*. Gianluca walked towards her, his eyes crinkled at the sides with concern, his hand reaching for her even as she pulled away. She was vaguely aware of her own voice muttering an apology, excusing herself on the pretence of using the bathroom.

Once she was in the hallway, she quickened her pace, walking hard and fast in no particular direction at all. Her chest burned and inhaling each breath took a sudden effort as she had never experienced before. It felt as though she were underwater and fighting not to breathe in. She needed fresh air before her lungs burst open. The migraine that had been threatening all morning erupted with impressive force in her temples, bringing with it a wave of nausea that almost brought her to her knees. She stopped in an open doorway that led out onto the back gardens. The cool breeze in her face did nothing to abate the awful sense that her legs were about to completely give out from underneath her. She needed to calm down, she needed to...

Unable to stand a moment longer, she felt her body slide parallel to the door until she was suddenly sitting down on cold, hard tiles. The blue of the sky seemed to blend into the green of the grass, colours jumping and mixing with one another to form a kind of Impressionist painting rather than reality. A shadow in the distance moved closer, and a rough shout sounded very close by. She was vaguely aware of strong arms lifting her, pulling her against a familiar hard, warm chest.

She shook her head, hearing a guttural demand for an ambulance seemingly coming from far away, though, when she looked up, Nysio held her tightly in his arms.

'Tell me what is happening, *tesoro*,' he pleaded, his face pale under his swarthy tan.

'Nysio,' she murmured, shocked at how weak and thready her own voice sounded. 'There's something very wrong.'

CHAPTER THIRTEEN

NYSIO WAITED PATIENTLY. His eyes completely focused on the door that a team of doctors had disappeared through along with Aria. He was vaguely aware of Eros and Priya seated across from him, worry evident on their faces. Xander and Pandora had stayed at the *palazzo* to tend to their guests, which he was immensely grateful for. He felt like a caged animal, unable to stop pacing the length of the waiting area. He had practically growled when the doctors said they all needed to leave the room in order for them to properly examine the patient. His chest went painfully tight as he remembered the sight of Aria hooked up to tubes on the hospital bed. She had been unconscious for barely a minute, but still…

A man in a white coat exited the room and Nysio stood straight, aware of the others moving to attention as well.

'Is one of you the next of kin?' the doctor asked.

Both Nysio and Priya stepped forward, answering yes simultaneously.

'I meant the baby's father?' the doctor said, unaware of the sudden tension.

'That would be me,' Nysio said.

'The…baby? Aria is having a baby?' Priya eyed him in shock.

Nysio ignored her. 'Is Aria okay?'

'Ms Dane is suffering from acute anaemia and low blood pressure, not uncommon in the first trimester. Her iron levels are incredibly low so we will be admitting her overnight for observation. She lost consciousness for a short time, as you witnessed today. She's going to need an iron infusion, but I believe that, once she's had it, she'll be fine as long as she's careful.'

Nysio felt relief flood him, his fists loosening by his sides. 'And the baby…'

The doctor removed a sonogram from his clip chart, holding out the blurry black and white image. 'It's still early, but from what I can tell, the pregnancy is at about nine weeks gestation and both babies are developing nicely according to the dates.'

'Both…babies?' Nysio froze, his hand seeming to reach out of its own volition, grabbing the sonogram from the doctor's hands. He absorbed the news, relief flooding him that Aria was going to be all right. But there were two babies. Two.

The doctor had him sign a few forms before saying they could go in and see Aria once the nurses had finished the infusion. Nysio still stood there, staring down at the two barely visible white shadows on the small sonogram in his hands. He traced one finger across each blob, amazed at the fierce urge to protect them with all of his might. He would protect their mother too, he silently vowed. Even from himself.

After a couple of minutes of tense silence, the nurse emerged and ushered them into the private room. Aria lay propped up on pillows in the large white bed, tubes in her arms connecting her to various medical devices that surrounded her. Nysio felt a lump in his throat, as Priya rushed forward and gently embraced her friend.

After a moment of inaudible sobbing, the women separated and Priya shook her head sharply. 'I can't believe you kept this big a secret from me.'

Eros stepped forward from where he had been hovering in the doorway, and Nysio felt enormous gratitude towards his brother as he gently suggested to his wife that they leave Aria to rest. Nysio simply nodded once, a silent thanks to the family member he'd never believed he would have. The family member that Aria had given him really, through her encouragement to reconnect with both his brothers ever since she'd found out about them.

And then they were gone, and the room was finally silent except for the soft beeping of the machines she was hooked into. He looked at her then, really looked at her. She looked so pale and exhausted in the hospital bed, her hands clutching the blankets as though she held on for dear life.

'I'm sorry about all of the drama,' she said, twisting the hospital bracelet on her wrist. 'You heard the doctor, the babies are fine, there's two of them… And I just need some extra iron… Probably because there's two of them, did I mention that there's two?'

Nysio tried to smile, but felt an uncomfortable lump growing in his throat as he took a seat on the edge of the bed. 'I guess that answers my next question, if you were surprised.'

'I was so scared.' Her voice cracked. 'I'd been working too hard on my plans for the line, forgetting to take my vitamins and then there was all the sex… I was so sure that there was something terribly wrong.'

'Time has never moved slower than that half-hour today as I tried to get you here.' He shook his head. 'I thought…'

'I know,' Aria whispered. 'I thought the worst too. I had been getting the migraines and dizzy spells all week. I should have got checked sooner. I'm just not quite used to being cared for quite so much.'

'Well, you should be,' he said soberly. 'You have two babies to grow now, which means you need to be watched more closely. You're going to need to take it easy for a while.'

Aria sat upon the bed, twisting the cover in one hand. 'I know. I realise now that I hadn't fully accepted the pregnancy. I was distracting myself with all the wrong kind of worries. Rather than worrying about myself and the physical challenge of growing a child inside me.'

'Two children,' Nysio said pointedly.

'Yeah…' Aria shook her head. 'I think I'm still processing that part, to be honest. Are you as terrified as I am?'

Nysio was quiet. He stood up, walking over to the large window and bracing his hands on the ledge. 'I think today has made it more real for me too. Of the plans we need to make and decide upon. Now that we know the pregnancy will need extra care.'

'Yes… I know.'

'Right now, you need to rest.' Nysio placed his hand over hers and felt his heart squeeze when she gripped onto him so tightly. He wanted nothing more than to hold her tight enough that she could never get free again. He wanted to wrap her in luxury and care and attention, and stand in front of anyone who intended her harm. He wanted to give her everything. But she didn't want it from him.

'They said that you can leave by tomorrow, but I called Priya to see if you could stay with her.' He removed his hand, shoving his fists into his pockets to force himself not to reach out again. 'I assumed you'd want your space to make your plans.'

Nysio hardly noticed his surroundings as he walked out of the hospital room and left three quarters of his heart behind him. The terrible reality had already begun to dawn on him that the most selfish thing that he could possibly do would be to keep her and their children by his side. Aria was not built to live in his cage. She was too vibrant, too full of life and love to be imprisoned in the world into which he had been born. All along he had told himself he needed to keep her, to convince her to parent their children together and do the best for the Bacchetti legacy.

The thought of letting her go killed him, but he would do it if it meant seeing her smiling and happy. He could be selfless for her. He could show her his love that way...because he knew with certainty that he must be in love. Nothing else could possibly hurt this much. He sat in his car, feeling the silence cocoon him, but it gave him no comfort as it usually did. He had grown to adore all the noise and movement and unpredictability that came with loving Aria Dane.

CHAPTER FOURTEEN

THE NEXT TWENTY-FOUR hours passed quickly as the hospital staff performed numerous checks to make sure that it was okay for Aria to be discharged from their care.

Aria sat up in the bed, as she took in the two identical blobs for the thousandth time. Those blobs were inside her, she thought with a sense of awe. Until now, this pregnancy hadn't seemed real yet. Obviously, she knew she was pregnant and would eventually give birth. But she hadn't really given thought to the fact that there was an actual life forming and growing inside her. There had seemed too much else to consider. But when the doctor had placed the ultrasound wand on her stomach and she had heard those two little hearts beating slightly out of time with one another... Nothing else had seemed more important.

She leaned back on the pillows, placing both

of her hands on her slightly rounded stomach and closed her eyes. 'I know you guys are probably much too small to hear me,' she said softly. 'I'm sorry if things got a little crazy in there lately. I've been making myself far too busy. But you're going to be my priority now.'

Priya was surprisingly patient when Aria arrived at her hotel. She listened as Aria talked about what had occurred in the weeks since her friend's failed wedding and her reappearance, and Priya shared her own story.

It surprised Aria deeply to learn that Priya had trusted Eros so blindly, but then she realised that she was not so different herself. She had done exactly the same thing, had she not? She had taken one look at Nysio and wanted him badly, so she'd jumped into bed with him the first chance that she could. Or jumped onto a bathroom vanity counter, whatever! Priya's eyes widened when Aria shared that particular story. She wasn't ashamed of her actions. She'd always shared everything with Priya, after all. But things were different now, Priya was in love and somebody's wife. She had plans for the future. Aria was still adrift.

'You could set up your business wherever

you are; why don't you come back to New York with me?'

Aria thought about it, thought about taking Priya's offer and going ahead with her plan to start up a small lingerie label. But the thought of embarking upon the pipe dream that she had rolled over for so long suddenly had absolutely no pleasure in it.

'No… The time isn't right, I think,' she said, lowering her hand to her stomach where her two little beans were safely nestled. 'I got a scare, thinking something was wrong with the babies. I think I want to stay here, in Florence, for a bit. Here is where I'm going to live. I want the babies to be near their father…and I want to be near him too.'

She hadn't realised that was how she felt until the words left her lips. When she said them aloud, she knew it was true, she knew it was what she wanted. Stay here with Nysio, to raise their children near their grandmother and grandfather who had already shown more love and excitement at the babies' existence than even she had.

'Have you told Nysio that?' Priya asked, a strange look in her eyes.

'I haven't seen him since yesterday; I think

he's been avoiding me. We had a fight. He asked me to marry him and I said no.'

Priya's face stiffened with surprise. 'Oh. That probably didn't help you to relax.'

'But now I've thought about it, I think I've been an absolute fool. He's amazing, Priya, and I think I've been completely unfair to him and allowed my own wounds to still dictate my life. I think… I think I at least owe it to myself and my babies to try.'

'I should tell you that Eros had a meeting with Nysio and Xander this morning. He told me that your baby daddy was planning to do something big with them. Something about getting balance?'

Aria sat up straight. 'What does he mean?'

'I'm not sure… I only know that he said that it was for his family, so I didn't question it. But Eros seemed stunned on the call, and he asked Nysio if he was sure he could part with so much history.'

His history. His place as legitimate heir. Aria felt her stomach drop. What had he done?

'I actually can't believe he would do something like that for me without talking to me first. I have to go.' She stood up and moved, grabbing her bags and hastily throwing in her belongings.

'Slow down, you've just got out of the hospital,' Priya begged.

'I'm not on bed rest, I'm quite able to go downstairs and get into a cab.' She closed her eyes, placing a hand on her chest as she felt a panicked sob pass through her. 'I've made so many mistakes; I need to go to him. I need to make this right or I'll never forgive myself.'

'Okay, but at least take my car. Being lovesick makes you crazy apparently,' Priya said, smiling. 'But I can see why you love him. I see the way he looks at you too, the way he cared for you in the hospital. I think you know what you want now, so go and get him.'

Aria still couldn't believe what Nysio was telling her, as they stood once more in the centre of the maze at the *palazzo*, where she'd found him.

'I realised that I don't want my children to be raised under the same weight of expectation that I was,' he was saying. 'I don't want them to have that life.'

He moved away from her and she felt something tense within, urging her to move closer, to hold him to her, but she held back.

'So you just…gave it all away? The Bacchetti part of your wealth?'

'I've given it back to the people who treasure it most: the people of Florence. I've set up a charity for the benefit of our community and all funds will go to those in need. They can also open the *palazzo* to the public; you were right that the treasures inside should be seen and admired.'

'It's a wonderful thing to do,' she said approvingly.

'For decades I hid myself within these walls, working myself to exhaustion just to try to prove that I was worthy of the Bacchetti name I had been born with. But then I met you...' He smiled at the memory. 'You made me remember what it felt like to feel free. Then I brought you here and you made me see it for what it was. A prison of my own making. I believed I had no choice but to continue clinging to the reputation that my father had guarded so fiercely. I believed that I owed it to him and to my mother. You made me see that what I wanted mattered too.'

She smiled tremulously back at him.

'Once upon a time, being a Bacchetti was everything that I was. I was raised to be the heir to a dynasty that spanned generations. It was a duty that I performed happily, because it made my father proud. I idolised him. But I know now that love doesn't always mean having to live up to other people's expectations.'

'Oh, Nysio…'

'I'm not trying to change your mind about marrying me. You've made it very clear why you don't want to. I did this for me. I did this because you made me realise where my true passion lies. I never actually wanted to be the man that my father raised me to be. I never cared all that much about being a Bacchetti. You made me remember the person I had once wanted to be until my guilt forced me back into a role I felt duty-bound to accept. I don't think I truly knew who I was for a very long time.'

'I know who you are,' she said gently.

'When you came to my rescue on that street in Manhattan, I thought at first it was just attraction, lust. It was easy to disregard the raw need within me that refused to let you go, easy to brush it off as amazing chemistry but nothing more.'

'To be honest, I felt the same thing.'

'I thought I was rescuing you, the day we met. You were abandoned, alone and afraid and yet…you wound up being the one to rescue me. You brought something back to life in me the moment you commanded me to look in your eyes and breathe. That was the moment

I felt that shift within me from simply exist-
ing to wanting more. That was the moment I
fell in love with you, Aria Dane. I think a part
of me has felt it all along and it terrified me.
I brought you to my palace like a prize that I
feared someone would come along and take
away. I have made so many mistakes with you,
tesoro. I cannot undo the things that I've said
that have made you feel trapped. I never want
you to feel trapped, Aria, never. I love you too
much.'

Aria felt a burst of emotion choke her, the
weight of his revelations pressing down upon
her as her hand instinctively dropped to cradle
her stomach and the precious cargo that nestled
within. While she had been lying in her hospital bed feeling slightly sorry for herself, he
had been busy acknowledging the cracks in his
foundations and setting about doing the work
to make himself whole again.

She remembered what he had told her of his
life, the man he'd been raised to be. She knew
that he'd never truly wanted it, had seen how
much it took from him every time he played
the part that had been assigned to him. She had
witnessed his passion when they were in Sardinia, his love for the wine and the people who
made it, but she had never truly believed that

he would listen to her. That he would finally choose balance for himself.

'I haven't done any of this in order to convince you to marry me. You helped me to see that our children would be more affected by me remaining here…in this palace, than by being born in or out of wedlock. I don't know how else to explain it, I'm just…'

'You're choosing the path that will make you the best version of you,' she finished for him.

'Yes…that's exactly it.' He blinked, then a smile transformed his face. If the smile he'd given her that night when she'd played the piano for him had been like fireworks…this one was a full-on explosion. His eyes shone and gone were the shadows that she'd grown so used to trying to coax away. He didn't need her to coax them away, he was shining through his own darkness just fine. The realisation made a little part of her ache. But the thought of him living that life to the fullest without her being the woman standing by his side was suddenly utterly ridiculous.

She closed her eyes, fear and uncertainty clogging her throat as emotion finally won the battle and put an end to her composure. Tears filled her eyes and she shook her head, turning away from him, trying to hide her own weakness.

He moved towards her in an instant, as she knew he would, strong hands encircling her shoulders and pulling her back tightly against his chest.

'Damn hormones,' she gasped, grateful that he was still behind her and that he couldn't see her ugly cry.

'Why do you insist on hiding your vulnerability from me? Do you fear that I can't take it? Because I assure you I can. I will be here to support you over these next months, no matter how hard it gets. That was never an option. You may have refused my proposal, but I never intended to walk away from you. Never, *tesoro*. I only want your happiness, whether that is being with me as my wife, or simply as the two primary caregivers for these two incredibly lucky children that are growing inside you.' His hand drifted down, covering hers gently, reverently.

'I know I hurt you when I refused your proposal,' Aria said. 'And once I'd realised what a mistake I had made, I was worried it was too late. I knew I'd messed up but had absolutely no idea how to put it right.' She felt his breath on the crown of her head and could hear the steady thump of his heartbeat directly behind hers. He was holding her so tightly, but not inappropriately so, she could feel him holding back from crossing that line. A line that seemed so utterly ridiculous to her now that she could see what she needed to say and do so clearly.

Honesty. Trust. A leap of faith.

She turned around in the circle of his arms, realising that she had run from her own feelings long enough and her children deserved for her to be brave. To believe that he loved her. To fight for their family, the one that she truly wanted for them.

Aria met his gaze, her voice shaky. 'There is more I need to say, so much more that I want to say… I just can never seem to get the words out the right way when it's important. When I have you looking at me, all the words pile together and I…'

'How about if I close my eyes?'

She gasped, stunned once again at how easily this man took care of her. How ridiculous it had been for her to run away from his natural protective nature when it lit her up inside like this. His eyes fluttered closed and it took all of her strength not to just rush past the words that needed to be said and simply kiss him until neither of them could breathe. But kissing had never been something they needed to work on together.

Communication first, she reminded herself. Kissing later.

'Nysio, I think I've deliberately kept you at arm's length because I was afraid of my own feelings after what Theo did to me. I also thought that what I needed to gain self-respect was to push myself as hard as I could to succeed at a career. I wanted to feel capable and worthy of the life growing inside me. Both of them.'

She stopped for a moment and he smiled encouragingly at her, still with his eyes shut.

'The past few days have just become a haze of brain fog. The scare that we had, worrying that something terrible had happened to the babies... It made me realise that I was running in entirely the wrong direction.' Once again she placed a hand over her stomach where the tiny lives within her were growing steadily and healthily. 'I don't think that I truly processed what was actually happening until I thought it had been taken away from me. I've always been different from the rest of my family, and I've felt ashamed that I've struggled so much. I've always judged myself far more harshly than anyone else ever has. And when you proposed to me…when I said no to you, and it felt like my heart was breaking in two… I knew I was in way deeper than I'd thought I ever could be.'

'I know Theo destroyed your trust,' he said gently.

She winced. 'I didn't think I'd ever be able to trust anyone again enough to marry them.' She forced the words out past the lump in her throat. 'I figured I'd only be setting myself up for failure and abandonment. That I was better off alone. But then you came into my life and for the first time I found myself actually wanting more…and it terrified me. So when we found out about the pregnancy, it was the easiest thing in the world to put on my armour again. It's so much harder for me to be vulnerable…to allow myself to hope. But the more I thought about it, the more I realised that I wanted nothing more than to be married to you. To wake up in your arms every morning and be surrounded by our beautiful children, wherever that may be.'

He opened his eyes and smiled down at her.

'I love you too,' she said, meeting his gaze and not letting go. 'I want everything that you have to offer me, Nysio. I really don't care where we are living, or what life looks like, so long as we're together.'

'*Dannazione*, I don't have the ring on me.' He looked flustered, a small blush appearing on the tops of his cheeks, something that made her smile wide and soft and lean even further into him. She wanted to draw pictures of this man and take photos of him and just stare at him all day. Hardly believing that he was truly hers, that he truly loved her as deeply and unconditionally as she loved him. Because she could no longer deny that that was the truth. He had given up more than anyone she had ever known; he had walked away from a fortune and a status that had given him a riches and power beyond most people's dreams.

'I don't need a ring,' she said, emotion forcing the words out in an unsteady cadence. 'So long as I have you in my heart and in my arms, I need nothing more.'

'I know you don't need a ring, but I'll still be giving it to you. Consider it an echo of my archaic caveman. I want everyone to know that you are mine, just as I am yours.'

'You know… I really do like the sound of that,' she said huskily, 'but if you get to show everyone that I'm yours, perhaps I should brand you in return?'

'What exactly did you have in mind?'

'A tattoo perhaps.' Her voice was a soft murmur as she trailed a finger up his sternum, his throat and then up past his lips and nose to point at his head. 'Right in the centre of your forehead.'

He laughed, a sound she'd once thought she might never hear again and now it came from him so easily. She silently vowed to make him laugh like this every day for the rest of their lives.

'Will you brand me with your name?' he asked, stroking a hand down her ribcage. '*Property of Aria. Do Not Touch*?'

'Property is a word just so devoid of passion. I was thinking more along the lines of *Taken by Aria... Possessed by Aria... Beloved by Aria.*'

'I really like the sound of that last one.' The hint of humour had left his voice, and he suddenly sounded hoarse with desire. In one rapid movement he was gathering her deeper into the circle of his arms so that every inch of their bodies touched from chin to knee and suddenly Aria's mind was only focused on getting as much of his delicious body under her palms as she could manage. Their kisses were slow and sensuous, filled with the whispered promises of their future and even a few tears on her part.

'So if you've given this place away to your

charity now, to open up to the public…does that mean that you're essentially homeless?'

He raised a wicked eyebrow. 'I'm still in possession of a rather sizeable fortune, an entire stockbroking company, not to mention a billion-euro wine label.'

'Oh, you poor man. Just the one wine label?' She tutted. 'Sounds like you're in need of rescue.'

'Miss Dane… Are you wondering about the fastest way to get your fiancé into bed?'

Her fiancé. She had once thought that word would hold nothing but bad memories for her for ever, but now, looking at this man, she felt only excitement for the future, and the absolute certainty that it would be wonderful.

'My fiancé should know by now that I am utterly insatiable when it comes to celebrating moments. And this definitely feels like something we should be celebrating. In an aeroplane bed, on a bathroom sink, in a gazebo… I don't particularly have a preference for the location. But I'm pretty sure that if we don't get all of our clothes off in the next five minutes, I won't be held accountable for my actions.'

'I suppose I should take you seriously…'

'Always.'

EPILOGUE

ARIA SIGHED AND tilted her head up to let the Greek sun warm her face for a moment. The small beach was a quiet respite from the noisy house party up above while Nysio chased around after their twin boys, Emilio and Mauro. They had been guests on Eros and Priya's private island paradise for the past two days and it had been just what they'd all needed. Her decision, backed by Nysio, to go ahead and take the leap and start up her own line of lingerie while pregnant had seemed utterly ridiculous at the time, and even more so when the orders had begun flooding in and they'd had to increase their warehouse size three times. But they still prioritised family time above all else.

'There you are.' A familiar voice spoke from the wooden stairway above, and she looked up to see Priya making her way down, her four-month-old baby daughter, Amara, in her arms.

'I swear, if one more person asks me where my husband is, I'll scream.'

Aria smiled as her best friend came to sit beside her on the loveseat, her tiny daughter kicking and cooing in her arms. Aria instantly put her arms out to take her goddaughter, grinning when the baby gave her a gummy smile in response.

'Amara, tell your mama it's time for her to come and live in Italy,' she said.

'Amara, tell your godmother that if she wants to hold a baby more often, she has a very handsome husband who is more than willing to oblige her,' Priya teased.

'I'm so going to tell Nysio you called him handsome.'

'You seem to forget that time you asked my husband if he would be interested in modelling for one of your ad campaigns.'

'She asked Xander too.' A quiet voice came from behind them and they both turned to see the familiar smile of Xander's wife, Pandora, as she came into view.

'Okay, this is beginning to feel like a pile-on,' Aria grumbled good-naturedly, shifting over to make room. 'And yes, when it comes to business, I admit I'm a little bit shameless.'

'A little bit?' Both women laughed aloud,

making the baby jump with surprise in her arms. Aria shushed them, rocking the small bundle in her arms with ease.

Aria stared down into her goddaughter's big brown eyes and almost felt a momentary pang of longing strike her.

'I know that look.' Priya smirked. 'Changed your mind on having more babies?'

'Not a chance.' Aria laughed and stood up, swaying from side to side, and hummed a little bit of one of the Italian nursery rhymes her mother-in-law had taught her. Her muscles remembered doing this, night after night when both of the twins had developed colic at the same time.

Nysio had held one and she'd held the other and some nights they'd both fallen into bed exhausted, only to be pulled awake again a short time later. She had no shame in admitting that the first year of parenting had brought her to the brink of her own limits. But that wasn't the reason why they'd decided they were content with their little family as it was. It was simply something they'd both discussed and unanimously agreed upon. Two was their number.

Their boys would turn four soon and they adored being parents and couldn't wait to see what wild times lay ahead. She had loved watching Nysio find his way as a new father and had felt his support as she did the same. They had a beautiful balance in life that meant they could do things like sail off to Greece for this past week. They had also taken a long-overdue honeymoon last year when Nysio had sailed them on a romantic week exploring the Mediterranean for their second wedding anniversary.

She still laughed every time she remembered how long she'd made him wait before finally getting married. It had been a running joke amongst him and their new extended family that Nysio had been the only brother not to marry in a rush after that fateful jilted wedding, despite being the first to become a father. So when the time finally came, Aria had suggested they play a trick on their loved ones, inviting them all to a party where they joined the brothers' anniversary club as a surprise.

Their wedding had taken place exactly two years after the mile-high night that had bound them for ever, in the centre of the maze where he had first told her he loved her.

'I'm actually pregnant.' Pandora blurted.

Priya and Aria both froze and looked down at the third sister of their slightly unconventional extended family set.

'Oh, my God, did I just say that out loud?' Pandora clapped a hand over her mouth. 'Oh, no, I promised Xander that I wouldn't tell anyone yet. It's really early.'

'My lips are sealed.' Priya beamed, reaching out to give her a one-armed hug. 'But now you get the honour of minding Amara for practice while I go meet Eros at the dock.'

'No funny business!' Aria shouted at the rapidly shrinking silhouette of her best friend as she practically ran down the beach towards the opposite end of the island where the small dock resided. Aria looked down to find Amara's head lolling slightly as Pandora tried to get a handle on the active infant. Aria smiled, carefully helping to readjust the baby's head.

'I don't even know how to hold a baby.' Pandora groaned, shifting the little girl's weight awkwardly into her elbow. 'I have absolutely no idea what I'm doing.'

'Neither did I, back when Emilio and Mauro were born,' Aria confessed to the woman who had joined her life as a sister-in-law but had quickly become one of her best friends. 'You must remember the day of their christening when I almost dropped one of my sons in the font?'

Pandora laughed at the memory. 'Oh, yes… I'd almost forgotten that.'

'I was so nervous, having so many family members watching me. I was a wreck as a parent most of the time at the start, but I found my way.'

'I wouldn't mind skipping ahead to this stage.' Pandora gestured to the party above.

Aria looked up at the party, spying the familiar broad silhouette of the man she loved up on the deck above them. Two tiny heads bobbed on either side of him as the boys jumped and called for her and Pandora to come and join them. She waved, feeling her heart thump painfully with so much love.

'The hard times are made easier with the right person by your side. I promise.'

Nysio sneaked a look at the two little boys resting peacefully in their bunk beds on the yacht and sighed with relief. Asleep at long last. The impromptu football game with Zio Eros and Zio Xander had been the perfect way to end their weekend, but the excitement had made the boys even more difficult to get to sleep than usual. Still, he'd never tire of the sight of seeing his wealthy and powerful half-brothers felled by the boundless energy of the Bacchetti twins.

He smiled and wondered what the all-powerful Zeus would think, knowing that his attempt to pit his sons against one another in a race to inherit had only succeeded in bringing them together. Their joint charity efforts were now numerous and they met regularly for family gatherings. A shadow in the doorway made him pause, and he looked to see his wife watching him as he gently tucked the duvet around both boys and tiptoed backwards from the room.

'That was a long day,' he said, once the door was safely closed behind them. 'I never thought I'd say this, but I think this age might be the hardest yet.'

Aria's brows rose in disbelief. 'Harder than the potty-training stage?'

'They couldn't run quite so fast back then.'

The medium-sized yacht had been one of his best purchases in the four years since Aria Dane had walked into his life. Dinner was a beautiful cheeseboard with a side of homemade crusty bread gifted to them by Eros and made with all local ingredients. They ate in companionable silence out on the top deck, accompanied by nothing other than the sound of the waves and the small flickering light of the baby monitor.

Nysio was content. An emotion he'd never thought he might claim for himself. Gone were the constant stomach aches and the need for rigid routine and control. It hadn't disappeared fully, of course, he was still a creature of habit and ferociously dedicated to the three-day working week he'd adopted for himself. A life of balance suited him beautifully, he'd soon discovered. Travelling the world had never been a part of his plans but every time he watched his wife's eyes light up exploring a new city, he felt a peace as he'd never known before.

She'd given this to him, this powerful, beautiful warrior of a woman who had come bursting into his life like a comet, changing everything for evermore.

'You're looking strangely at me again,' Aria said. 'What are you thinking?'

'I'm not thinking, I'm living,' he answered honestly.

'Ah yes, living in the moment. Glad you thought of that one, babe.' She rolled her eyes, then squealed when she seen his brows raise in dark challenge.

Nysio pounced, gripping her around the waist and pinning her between him and the yacht's galley-kitchen counter. Aria made a weak attempt at wriggling away before relaxing into his hold, smacking him lightly on the shoulder for good measure.

The scent of her wild-summer-berry shampoo filled his nose and he groaned, taking a single playful nibble of her earlobe before whispering softly, '*Bellezza*…must you take credit for everything?'

'Yes, I must when I am the one responsible for the vast majority of wonderfulness that we experience every day. Case in point, the two little hellions currently asleep next door.'

'I agree on that point.' He smirked. 'Considering they both clearly take most of their fiery temperament from their mother.'

She lunged for him, but he turned her playful attack into a passionate embrace that quickly escalated until they were both suddenly tearing each other's clothes off and he was laying her out on the galley floor.

'You know how I feel about these wrap dresses,' he groaned, pulling at the tie sash at her waist. One pull and the material fell open, revealing her signature strawberry-printed silk lingerie. 'You are like a prize I've been waiting to unwrap all day, *dolcezza*.'

'Spoken like a true ship's captain.' She laughed, then writhed as his hands traced the outline of her breasts. 'Sometimes I wonder if you love these gifts more than you love me.'

'You're jealous?' He growled playfully, nipping at the soft supple skin along the edge of the delicate fabric. 'You need me to show you how much I adore all of you?'

'Perhaps. Can you do that for me, *amore mio*?' She smiled, knowing full well how much it affected him to hear her speak his native language.

'*Sì, tesoro.*' Because that was what she was: his greatest treasure.

Only when she was fully bared to him did he fulfil his promise, showing her exactly how much he appreciated every one of her gifts. Each touch an unspoken promise that he would never stop ensuring that she felt the full extent of his love for her, for ever and always.

* * * * *

Couldn't get enough of
Pregnant in the Italian's Palazzo?
Then make sure to dive into the
first and second instalments in
The Greeks' Race to the Altar trilogy
Stolen in Her Wedding Gown
The Billionaire's Last-Minute Marriage
Both available now!

And don't miss these other stories
by Amanda Cinelli!

The Secret to Marrying Marchesi
One Night with the Forbidden Princess
Claiming His Replacement Queen
The Vows He Must Keep
Returning to Claim His Heir

Available now!